THE ROOTS IN YOUR BONES

SAMANTHA EATON

ISBN-13: 979-8-9867247-2-0

Also by Samantha Eaton

The Insatiable Hunger of Trees

DEDICATION

For those who get us through, whether they are human or animal. Especially, for Jola.

CONTENT WARNINGS

The Roots In Your Bones contains the following potential triggers: centipede related body horror, gaslighting, suicidal ideation, disordered eating, exploration of divorce related grief, animals in brief peril, wildfire, intrusive thoughts, death, alcohol abuse, domestic abuse, murder, violence. If you are sensitive to any of these topics, please proceed with caution.

CHAPTER

ONE

THE CAT HASN'T STOPPED YOWLING SINCE WE LEFT Buffalo at six o'clock this morning, and all the ways I've tried to drown him out have failed. The guttural, distressed noises from the bottom of the void that is Beef have defeated all other sounds—white noise, audiobooks, and increasingly heavy genres of music—and some hours ago I decided my SUV is a type of purgatory for the lukewarm sins I've committed.

"Beef! Good god, can you please stop? Aren't you tired?" I groan.

We haven't interacted with another human since the Dunkin Donuts in one of the lower New England states. I say "we" because Beef gave the kid an earful, despite the offering of a plain donut hole. I don't think drive through attendees usually give cats donut holes, but, in all fairness, the kid probably mistook Beef for a raccoon. He could easily pass as one. A chunky, solid gray raccoon with grabby little cat hands and a tendency for spelunking in the trash bin for a scrap of cheese. Checks out, really.

The iced coffee I bought has been long gone for hours now, but I still bring the straw to my lips and slurp the melted ice from the bottom of the cup. Even that dwindles. Fuck, I'm thirsty. And tired. And honestly not quite sure if I'm still even in the United States.

Inside my SUV, it smells like burnt coffee and fast food, and the heat barely creaking from the blowers only makes everything worse. It feels like I'm inside the vehicle equivalent of an armpit. I flip the temperature dial to the blue side and roll the window down an inch in hopes of freshening the air a little. Beef complains again. He objects by crying like a spoiled toddler, loud and dramatic and otherwise fine by all accounts.

The ocean lies to my right, not the clear blue water lined with white sand of the tropics, but a discontented shade of aqua that threatens an approaching storm. These waters sink ships.

My GPS yells at me from my phone, which has wound up lodged between the center console and my seat. I'd forgotten about the navigation. I've been on what seemed like the scenic route at first but ended up being the same not very scenic eastbound road for hours, so the mechanical voice startles me.

"In a quarter mile, turn left. Then, make a slight right."

There is nothing to the left. Trees, sure. Moose, maybe. But no houses that I can see. Shit, the GPS is going to get me killed before I even have a chance to start my life over. Damn it, GPS.

"Turn left."

Beef yowls again. My pulse hammers in my throat from a mix of annoyance and anxiety when I miss the turn. It looks more like a driveway than an actual road, but a faded green street sign indicates I should have made the left.

The navigator tells me to make a u-turn, and I'm too tired to drive until the GPS finds another road to try. If there even is another one. With a better sense of where I need to go, I make the turn in a gravel pullout on the side of the road. Beef's carrier slides across the seat and bumps into the door, and he acts as if he's been punted. This is not the cat to take on a two day road trip. No matter what, we'll make a home here in Maine, because I am not taking this cat anywhere else.

After two more turns, the road deposits me in a clearing in the woods with nothing but a single house and low hanging fog like the ghosts I've been told live on this land. The building has a floodlight on the front to alert me of its presence in the early darkness of late winter. The number on the weathered, paint chipped mailbox matches the one Elise gave me: 264. The house, a little log cabin, looks in better shape than the mailbox and resembles the pictures she showed me, though I didn't realize it was this deep in the middle of nowhere. It's the only house for two miles, maybe more.

I should've expected seclusion after what she told me. After learning why it's empty and why the new owners are letting me live here for free. Housesitting, not charity. They don't want to be here, but they can't let it wither either. My desperation buys them time to figure out what to do about their haunted childhood home.

My worn, nearly bald tires crunch on the gravel driveway as I ease my overworked SUV to a stop, and I sit in the idling vehicle for a minute to text the one person I have left.

Marisa:
I made it to your great uncle's place.

Beneath the green text bubble, a message from Elise appears.

Elise:
Good! Now for a fresh start.

Marisa:
Thanks E. I owe you.

Elise doesn't respond before I jam the phone into the back pocket of my jeans and exit the car. I haul Beef's backpack type carrier onto my shoulders and drag my one suitcase full of clothes and a few meager possessions up the uneven stone path to the door.

As far as allegedly haunted or cursed houses in the woods go, this one only meets the single criteria of being far out in the middle of nowhere. Otherwise, it looks like a well-kept cabin. The outside is completely made from log, and a wreath of dried or dead flowers hangs on the neutral blue front door. The steps are made from sturdy wood, just like the porch that wraps around the front and one side of the house. A once manicured garden borders the porch, though the plants suggest they've been neglected for a while. Even in hibernation, they have grown into a tangle.

I find the key Elise told me about beneath a polished stone statue of a sleeping fawn, then let myself inside.

"Okay, bud. You're free." I set the carrier down on the floor.

Beef throws his body against the clear plastic orb at the top front of the carrier as if it will now let him through, not realizing I unzipped the sides for him to escape. Once he figures it out, he takes three steps, then turns on me with his signature poor, malnourished orphan baby face. He is the farthest thing from malnourished, but you try telling him that.

I check the carrier for mess, then set it in a corner beneath a set of key hooks in case he decides it is his safe place. The only thing left in the car now is cat food, a box of litter, and Beef's extra large plastic litter box, so I hurry out to get that and set it up. I can rest once the cat has food and a place to shit.

When Beef is situated, I wander the house that doesn't belong to me. It belongs to a dead man — Elise's great uncle, Roger. It worked out, in a bleak way, that I needed a place to go and Roger's remaining family didn't want to leave Texas or Arizona or whatever to come live in a cursed house. So here I am. It'll give me a few months to get on my feet, at least.

Roger's family must have hired someone to clean the place, because it doesn't look as though anyone had ever lived here. It feels like what I imagine a nice Airbnb to be like. Clean and cozy with a fridge and cabinets stocked with some basics. Nothing too expensive or elaborate, but also almost nothing that reflects the personality of whomever called the place home before I got here. It feels new, sterile, and I wonder if Roger would be sad to see it like this.

Despite the rumors Elise shared about the local legend of her great aunt killing someone here before disappearing herself, this place doesn't look haunted. It looks like a scene from a home decor magazine. Tidy and minimalist and strategically decorated to appear inviting even though no one lives here.

Maybe that's the point.

I imagine a vacationer would call it homey and comfortable, with the little accessories that look like they were purchased at TJ Maxx to add to the rustic, cabin vibe.

Wooden bowls and worn leather books fill space on an antique chest of drawers to one side. Fake hydrangeas in a gray and green ceramic vase. A map of the Maine coast hangs on the log wall above a stone fireplace.

Wandering on, I find one door locked—presumably a storage space—and then the master bedroom. It has a queen sized bed in the center with fresh linens and an apparently handmade quilt on it. There's a lamp made of polished, stacked stones set on a sturdy-looking nightstand that has books about the area stacked on the shelves beneath.

A door to the side, slightly ajar, leads to the bathroom and, oh god, the thought of a hot shower and then getting cozy in that bed sounds so good right now. Especially after spending a night in what could take the title as the Shadiest Motel In Buffalo New York™ with a very, very angry cat.

"Go take a shower, Marisa," I say. "Shower. Teeth. Sleep."

I rummage through my suitcase for clean underwear, pajamas, and my plastic grocery bag of toiletries, then make for the shower. As soon as the hot water hits my skin, I exhale the last eight years into the cloud of steam. I survived Chicago traffic. I survived a dirty murder motel. I survived twenty-four hours of driving spread across only two days.

I survived leaving the person I thought I was supposed to be beside forever.

Now, for the first time in a very long time, I am alone, and the weight of it on my shoulders feel so much lighter than I expected.

CHAPTER

TWO

I WAKE UP AS CLOSE TO ALONE AS BEEF WILL ALLOW. THE cat forms a lead weight against my stomach, a little cannonball instead of a little spoon, and he purrs like a lawnmower. He's warm in contrast with the brisk, vaguely pine scented air in the room around us, and I pull the covers closer to my face to preserve the coziness surrounding the rest of my body.

I have nowhere to be but here. I don't owe anyone but myself any of the hours in my day. This is my life now.

Other than Beef's purring, the house sleeps around us. The heavy quiet makes me uncomfortable. Every place I've ever lived has had something in the background—a wall that creaked when the wind blew just right, an ice maker that grumbled like an unfed stomach, the sound of traffic passing by too fast, the arguments of people in neighboring rooms or buildings. This house doesn't have any of that. This house has only silence.

It should be comforting. Should reinforce my belief that nothing lingers to haunt these walls. Perhaps I'm the ghost here with all the memories I want to bury.

I should get up and do something. My mind is still restless, hungry for a distraction. I came here for a fresh start, to build new relationships and make new friends, but my body wants to rest for a day to recover from the long drive and everything that came before it.

I could check out what the town has to offer, start looking for a job or a place to meet people my age at least. Getting a job won't be as bad as making connections. How do people even make friends after college? Everyone I know from back home had either faded into an old friend, or sided with Brent for one reason or another. Elise was a friend from work, but we never hung out aside from team gatherings where we'd drink vodka cranberry and talk about whichever coworker wasn't present. Typical work outing.

As much as I appreciate Elise, I'd like to find friends outside of whatever job I end up doing. Best not to shit where you eat, as they say.

The cat is the only meaningful thing I kept. Nothing else mattered. There wasn't even any money in leaving except my meager savings account that might barely get me through a month—three now, without having to drop a third of it on my half of the mortgage—and a couple thousand dollars from pawning my wedding and engagement rings the morning I left.

All I received was a packet of papers delivered by a police officer, neatly creased in the center, informing me my husband had decided to divorce me. No warning. No discussion. His face—neutral and collected—when I asked him about it still lingers in the back of my mind. It might stay there forever, even after days in the car trying to think of every possible reason I'll be better off.

"You should probably go," Brent had said as if I had anywhere to go. As if he hadn't been the one to choose the city, Madison, when I wanted to be closer to where I grew up in southeastern South Dakota. My only family, my dad, died two years ago from heart disease, so I had as much reason to return to South Dakota as I had to stay in Madison: exactly none.

So I let Elise talk me into quitting the mediocre-at-best office job we worked together and going on what she called a "grand adventure" across the country to find myself. It seemed like a reasonable enough idea. Elise is a persuasive enabler in the sense that all her ideas sound very good.

She told me about the rumors about her great aunt much later, when the plan had been solidified.

"Okay, B. I better get up and check this place out," I say.

The cat grumbles as I crawl out from underneath the covers. He doesn't move as I walk barefoot to the bathroom, but he watches me with slitted yellow eyes. How dare I disturb him. How dare I rob him of my body's warmth.

I dress in jeans that had fit me once, back when I had gym toned hips and legs, but now they hang loose at the thighs and sag in the seat. My green t-shirt fits baggy, as does the thick oatmeal colored men's cardigan I layer over it, and none of it is fashionably slouchy. Even my sense of style is tired. I don't remember losing the weight that once filled in these clothes, but it's been gone a long time.

Though, despite the lack of effort in my attire, my eyes look a bit brighter than they did a few days ago. That's got to count for something.

Once I'm dressed, I wander the house with a steaming mug of coffee cupped in my hands. The stainless steel coffeemaker was pristine, with the plastic still on the digital display and whomever prepared this house to be lived in — and someone absolutely had been hired for that, because this isn't how a dead man's house looks — left a bag of ground local roast in the cupboard above.

I examine the other photos on the walls, mostly framed prints of buoys and boats and other nautical things captured in black and white, and linger on an outlier: an out of focus picture of a vintage looking barn. A woman stands beside a split stall door, the top open to reveal a dark colored horse. She hugs the horse's head and looks utterly delighted in her early 90's style jeans and t-shirt and riding boots.

I envy the woman in the photograph so much it aches. Horses were always the perfect distraction from any problem I faced. I miss letting my mind suppress all thoughts unrelated to staying upright in the saddle. It's been so long.

In the bottom corner, "Evie, 1993" has been written in dark ink.

Another moment of taking in the scene in the photo, then I move on to take in the rest of the objects left out in the house. My hands trace the leather of the title-less books stacked on the chest of drawers beneath the poster of the coast.

One of them feels different than the other two. The leather softer, more worn and the spine cracked and split from use. A stain mars the front cover where something liquid had spilled. This thing didn't come from TJ Maxx. It belonged to someone.

The thought sends a ripple of unease through me, yet I feel compelled to read it.

My hand closes around the journal and I bring it towards me for closer inspection.

It's probably nothing remarkable. Perhaps a book of all Roger and his wife's friends. A photo album from all the points in their life they wanted to remember. An old recipe book passed down generations. The guestbook from their wedding.

I open the cover to the first page. The stain from the cover spreads across the bottom corner of the off-white paper. In the center of the otherwise blank page, there is a single line of half cursive, half print handwriting:

Property of Eveline Ouellette.

My blood goes cold for a moment, and I pull my phone from my pocket to text Elise.

> **Marisa:**
> Is Eveline the one who...
>
> you know

Elise had told me about the town's local legend involving her great aunt. I don't know whether she believes it herself, but she thought it was significant enough to tell me about in case the house turned out to be as haunted as rumors said.

> **Elise:**
> Yeah. Evie. Are people already asking about her? Seriously? How have you even encountered people this early?

> **Marisa:**
> I found her journal.

> **Elise:**
> Oh shit. I'm surprised the cleaners didn't pack it away with the rest of Roger's stuff.

What does it say?

As much as I ache for an answer, I resist turning to the second page. The book feels wrong. It radiates something — anger or sadness, though I don't know the difference between the two. It belonged to a woman who, regardless of what happened, was broken. Maybe Evie was like me once. Devastated and alone and wanting nothing more than a shred of hope to get her through the day.

Marisa: I don't know. I'll check it out later.

My priorities should be to get out of the house, check out the town, stop thinking about ghosts, maybe meet some people. One person would be sufficient, honestly. My priority is not reading the journal of a woman who's been missing for over ten years. A woman who, according to local legend, murdered a man and still haunts the place where it happened.

With the journal still in one hand, I notice the feeling of being watched. It comes from behind me, from the framed picture on the wall of Evie and her horse.

The presence of eyes locked on my back grows heavier, until I turn to meet the stare of the woman captured in a photo forever.

"She's not here," I tell myself. "Evie's gone."

The tingling discomfort of being observed insists otherwise.

CHAPTER

THREE

WHEN I DECIDE TO LEAVE, THE CAR GRUMBLES AS I TURN the key, then does the little shake it always does the first time I try starting it in the morning. Please, car, please hold on for a while longer. The Toyota is dying. It only needs to last long enough for me to get a job so I can actually justify buying a replacement.

A fifteen minute drive takes me to the center of town. Bowen's Leg, Maine is two and a half blocks of brick buildings, plus a volunteer fire department, a combination Dunkin Donuts and gas station that still has the manual pumps with numbers that flip as the price changes. Across from the older gas station is one more modern, with rival coffee chain Tim Hortons established inside. Beyond this cluster of town, a few buildings are visible a ways down the main stretch, and a blue sign with an H indicates a hospital straight ahead.

Okay, then.

This is Bowen's Leg. There is nothing here to explain a) why the town is called Bowen's Leg or b) what exactly people do for work here. Fish? Lumber? The hospital? I can't imagine anything beyond that, unless there's a hidden shopping center nearby where folks can secure minimum wage retail jobs.

I imagine myself on a boat, hauling cages of fish or crustaceans up from the bottom of the still-angry looking Atlantic, working until my hands no longer blister and my arms grow strong. There are guys barking orders and making comments, but not about me. On my fantasy boat, there is no sexism, only genuine appreciation of everyone's work.

"What a fuckin' dream, Marisa." I bark a laugh at myself. What a world it is inside my head.

Once I find a line of two-hour parking spots, I pull into one and take in my options. There's a bar named the Wobbly Leg, a restaurant called the Oceanside Diner, a tattoo parlor I very deeply hope is no longer in business and not just filthy, and a few professional offices. It seems too early to venture into what appears to be a dive bar and try making friends, so I go for the diner. Another cup of coffee can't hurt, if nothing else.

Inside the diner, there's a counter made of live edge wood with polished wooden stools lined up on one side, but, other than that, the rest of the interior looks cheap and antiquated. The countertop doesn't match the retro-because-we-couldn't-afford-to-upgrade style of the rest of the space, down to the worn tiles and booths with tears on the seats' vinyl and initials scratched into the surfaces of the tables.

A girl no older than eighteen with shiny, platinum hair and brownish-green eyes that match the crystal hung from a cord on her neck hands me a laminated menu and brings over a hot carafe of coffee, which she pours into a blue, ceramic mug.

"You're a new face," the girl says.

I glance at her, struggling to comprehend how she picked up on that so quickly.

"I am. Got in last night, actually."

The girl looks past me and out to the street, where her eyes settle on my parked car with its out of state plates. "Wisconsin? Wow. What brings you to Bowen's Leg?" She pronounces it *Bone's Leg* and has an accent that sounds like a shadow of the fake Boston accents on TV. Despite the enthusiasm in her tone, she doesn't come off bubbly or annoying and her voice sounds like its default state is bored.

"I'm housesitting for a friend of a friend while I get back on my feet. Thought I'd take the chance to test the healing properties of the ocean," I say.

She nods like I've given her the most interesting answer possible, and not only a shadow of truth.

The girl—Tanner, she tells me—keeps chatting while I nurse my second cup of mediocre diner coffee and pinch little bites from the blueberry filled croissant she recommended. She tells me how she wants to cross the country, how she's saving up to go to school in California even though she's not sure what to study.

"What do people do around here?" I ask as soon as I get the opportunity. "Where would I go to meet someone?" Fuck, that sounds like I'm looking for country Tinder. "Like make friends."

Tanner ponders for a second. "Everyone I know, I know from school which probably doesn't help you unless you want a bunch of dumb-ass kids for friends. I guess probably the Wobbly Leg is your best bet. You don't want to go on weekdays, or too early, or stay past midnight, or so I hear, but you might make some normal friends at happy hour."

I must make a face, because she holds her hands up in defense. "Not that I know from experience."

"It's fine if you do. I'm not your mom."

She lowers her hands and reaches for the carafe of coffee, but I shake my head. "I'm all set. Thanks for the advice," I say.

Tanner grins a wide smile. "Maybe I'll be a concierge in California."

"Well, here's another test for you then. Cat food. Where can I get it around here?"

"Oh my god, I want a cat." Her attention span sucks, but I take this statement as a request to see a picture, so I show her a couple photos of Beef. She proclaims her love for him by way of declaring she would die for him. "There's a little grocery store down past town behind the oil change place, or you could try the farm and garden store across from the hospital."

The words 'grocery store behind the oil change place' scream South Dakota and I feel utterly at home and nostalgic at the same time.

"Thanks." I hand her a ten dollar bill to cover the tab and a tip, then return to my car and head for the farm and garden store for cat food.

Before I leave my parking spot, I look into the glass front windows of the Wobbly Leg. This early in the morning, the interior is dark and eerie. Mason jars occupy the center of the tables in my line of sight, with nothing else as far as decoration, and the tall stools do look like they have at least one wobbly leg. I can't imagine it as a place I'd feel comfortable going on my own, at least not without pepper spray, but it might be my only option if I actually want to meet people. Tanner seems great, but she's right. I need people my age who've lost the optimism of dreams about California and a world full of opportunity.

Not much passes in the mile between town and the farm and garden store with its sprawling but mostly empty parking lot. I park between a rusty, beat up pickup truck and the most offensively orange Subaru wagon I've ever seen. Who chooses bright orange for their vehicle? What does bright orange say about a person other than 'please don't mistake me for a deer in the woods.'

"Can I help you find anything?" A guy in a dark green vest holding two tiny aloe vera plants in one hand appears in my path as soon as I enter the store. He has potting soil on his forehead from where he presumably pushed his dark, wavy hair out of his face, and a stupid smile that says *look how approachable I am in my little vest with these little plants.*

I would bet money on this guy being Bright Orange Car Guy.

"I'm looking for cat food."

He leads the way, stopping once at a desk in the center of the store to set the plants down, then takes me to an aisle dedicated to pet food. I find the brand and flavor Beef approves of, and pick up the biggest bag they have.

"Just what I needed," I say. "Um, also you have dirt on your forehead. In case you didn't know."

He glances up with brown golden retriever eyes as if he can see the smudge on his own forehead if he tries hard enough, then wipes at it with the back of his hand.

"Wow. Wonder how long that's been there."

I shrug. "At least it's just dirt." Oh my god. Did I seriously just make a thinly veiled poop joke? Kill me now. "I thought you'd probably want to know. You know?"

His smile widens, a bit less stupid looking and with little crinkles at the edges of his eyes. "I can't give you a discount, even if you did save me from looking like a dingus all day."

"Well, I guess next time I know to leave you to fend for yourself, since there's nothing in it for me."

Why am I doing this right now? Is this flirting? Am I *flirting?* I don't recognize myself. Never in my life would I have considered myself anywhere close to confident and capable of banter the way I am in this moment. This has to be a first. As soon as I notice though, I realize maybe I've laid it on too thick. I don't want to flirt with this guy, whose name tag reads JONAH in handwritten block letters, and I retreat into my default awkwardness.

"Damn, I thought I could count on you." Jonah doesn't seem to notice my retreat and keeps joking.

"I live to disappoint." For some reason, I offer a salute. Like some fucking Navy Seal. Jesus, Marisa. There is no middle ground between *almost flirting* and *woman who has never spoken to another human being ever in her entire twenty-six years on this earth.* Not for me, at least.

An unpleasant moment of silence passes while we head back to the register so I can buy this bag of food and leave with what's left of my dignity. Maybe there's an online course I can take on socializing, since I clearly cannot trust myself to behave like a functioning human.

"Well, thanks for the help," I say before practically lunging out the front door.

In the car, I deflate into the driver's seat and fold forward with my forehead on the steering wheel. I talked to people before, didn't I? Even if Brent got weird every time I said more than the absolute minimum to anyone, he was the one with the problem. Not me. He was the one constantly obsessing over whether my bisexual ass would run off with someone else at the first opportunity if he didn't take it upon himself to save me from myself.

Could he be why I'm like this? Insecure and unable to believe I know how to be around people?

I smack my palms against the steering wheel, pissed at Brent and pissed at myself for being such an idiot. Who would I be if I'd gone to a different college than him and we grew apart once the distance became too much? Or if I'd accepted the job I wanted up in Fargo and let him go to Madison on his own? How many of the pieces of myself I've lost could have been saved if things had been different?

I allowed this to happen to me.

My eyes prickle and my throat tightens, but I've cried enough for a lifetime so no tears come. I hit the steering wheel again, harder this time. My hands want to break something, to snap something in half or shatter it to a million pieces, but the wheel only absorbs the blow.

A knock comes on my window, two short thunks.

I glance up to see Jonah looking equal parts confused and concerned, so I crank the window down and offer a half-assed thumbs up.

"You forgot your card." He reaches through the window and hands me the debit card I'd presumably left in the store's chip reader.

"Oh. You're a life saver," I say, though the enthusiasm falls flat.

"You okay?" he asks. He looks like he genuinely cares. "Car trouble?"

"Oh. No, the car's fine. I'm fine. I just … I've had a rough couple of days." I brace for him to ask if I drove all the way here from Wisconsin, or some other question that has an easy answer I simply don't feel like thinking about right now because it could be the thing that breaks my fragile composure.

"I'm sorry."

I resist the instinct to tell him it's okay. It's not okay. Instead, I nod.

"I don't know what your situation is, and you don't have to tell me, but there's not a ton of people our age around here. If you want a friend …" Jonah seems to lose track of his thought for a second, then finds it again. "I'm not hitting on you or anything like that. It's just not every day I meet someone I could befriend, and you seem normal."

I blink at him. This is what I came here for: a friend.

So why am I not talking?

Is this how people make friends? Flat out asking them in a parking lot? I'll take it. I'll take this as a win.

Jonah keeps talking. "I have a couple friends, but two of them are my parents' age and the rest all have kids or got weird after getting married or divorced or shit like that."

I wince at the word *divorce.*

He didn't know. He couldn't have. Hearing it in this place I meant to make a sanctuary stings, though.

"Oh, you should set me up with them. A support group for tragedies. My husband — I guess ex, now — surprised me with papers on Thursday after we'd been together since high school." The words come out like bullets, or shards of glass. They hurt me, and they hurt Jonah too based on how he recoils.

"Shit." He sucks in a sharp breath, clearly feeling like a total asshole. "I'm sorry."

"I don't want your pity."

He pushes his hair out his face, making it stick up in chaos atop his head. "Okay. Fair enough."

This has gone so, so well, but despite the bumpy start, this guy seems okay. No serial killer vibes coming off him or anything like that.

I swallow the bitterness Jonah doesn't deserve.

"I'll take you up on your offer to be friends. It's been a while since I've had one of those."

It's still so hard to smile, to make the words sound light in contrast with the edge of the last ones I spoke. I offer my phone, open to the contacts list — a pathetic choice since it has literally three people in it and one is the Thumbs Down emoji.

He types a number in, then hands the device back to me and I text the number he put in.

"Nice to meet you, Marisa," he says. I realize I never told him my name until the *hi, it's Marisa!* text.

"That's me."

He nods. "I'm Jonah."

"Yeah. So says your name tag." I laugh weakly when he looks down to check. "You put yourself in here as Asshat."

"Well, you know … after my commentary, I figure you'll remember me as Asshat. I've proven myself as one whole hat for an ass."

"What the fuck, man?" I mutter, almost smiling. Almost.

"I promise I will not be an ass next time we talk."

"Sounds perfect," I say, half convinced I'll never talk to this guy again.

Before I roll the window back up, Jonah offers a hand —not for a handshake, but for a high five. A high-fucking five. Like we're in fifth grade and I just traded him a boss ass Pokemon card. What a dork. Still, I achieved what I came out here for.

CHAPTER

FOUR

THE SUN HAS BEGUN ITS DESCENT BY THE TIME I GET back to the house, and it feels surreal to return to a stranger's home. This place doesn't feel like where I belong yet, and I don't know if it ever will. This is temporary. A step along the path that leads to where I'm supposed to be.

My home wasn't in Madison with Brent. South Dakota feels as far away as a dream.

I interrupt my thoughts before I spiral too deep into my feelings. This is a start. The opening chapter in a sequel to the story I let die.

As I walk up the path to the front door, I notice a building at the far end of the yard. A barn. It's the barn from the photo in the house of the woman and the horse. It stands tall, boards grayed from years of weather, against the backdrop of trees. A line of wooden fencing circles a patch of dried grass, and within its perimeter are two split stall doors.

22

The fog must have hidden it when I arrived.

A string of wild turkeys wander beneath a section of fence, scouring the ground for something to eat. They cackle as they move, and I watch them for a while before my attention finds its way back to the barn.

The photo in the house showed Evie with a horse and this barn. I think about her, smiling and holding the horse's line loosely as they both posed for their picture. How did the woman who looked so happy turn into an alleged killer? And where did she go?

A chill runs through my body at the thought of the stories about Evie, and the journal inside calls to me. I want to know what she has to say.

At the door, heat blooms in my chest like blood dripping from a wound reopened before it could heal. Fuck. I grasp the doorframe to keep myself upright against the tingling sensation spreading over my whole body. Neon orbs burst behind my eyes and my head swims while the ground sways beneath my feet.

I forgot to eat lunch, and the croissant I picked at earlier has long left me, so I sink down and lean against the now closed door. My head pounds against the knees I rest it on, a pulse filling the emptiness of the house.

A scratching sound creeps into my brain like nails against the wall.

"Beef," I groan without lifting my head. "No clawing the wall."

The sound stops.

"Thank you."

A few more minutes pass before I feel stable enough to stand, then I make for the kitchen where there's a loaf of oatmeal bread in the freezer. I take two slices and pop them into the black toaster on the light marble counter. I don't think the appliance has ever been used. All other toasters

I've ever encountered have had years' worth of crumbs collected at the bottom, where this one only has a shiny, metal tray.

The scratching sound comes back, this time from a different part of the house.

"Beef!"

I look around for the cat, but he must be hiding somewhere like I won't notice he's up to no good. Typical.

The bread pops, not as browned as I'd like, but I remove it from the toaster anyway and smear peanut butter across the surface. I don't taste it as I practically inhale every last crumb, but I feel a bit better with the weight of it at the bottom of my uneasy stomach. I have to get better about this.

As I rinse the peanut butter off the knife, the damn cat starts on his bullshit again. It's Beef's signature series of three. He laps water in threes, scratches the box in threes, weighs three times the average cat.

Scritch scritch scritch.

"Cut it out, man."

I round the corner into the bedroom and find him napping in the center of the bed. Out cold.

The sound returns, this time outside.

Scritch scritch scritch.

I fling open the thick curtains but find nothing. The closest tree is far enough away that a stray branch couldn't possibly be tapping on the glass.

Scritch scritch scritch.

Now it comes from the front door, so I rush across the house and pull it open. Only the darkening night greets me. Nobody. Not a person. Not an animal or a particularly crisp fallen leaf.

"What the hell?" I ask the emptiness.

It's the woods, I remind myself. I'm not accustomed to

the woods. Before this, Brent and I lived on the edge of the city in Madison, and eastern South Dakota didn't have anything taller than the high prairie grass. The only time I ever saw a forest as dense as the one around me now, my dad and I had driven west to the Black Hills. We went to see the Badlands and Mount Rushmore and some caves, then stayed in Rapid City in a cheap roadside motel. The trees there had been so thick, they coated the landscape in a layer of dark forest so different from the yellows and browns of home.

Dad worked all the time since it was just him and me, so we didn't vacation much, so that made the trip west feel like the biggest adventure ever to ten year old me. I wonder what he'd think about me being all the way out here, mere miles from the ocean in a state we usually forgot about. Would he be proud of me, or would my circumstances disappoint him?

I realize I still stand in the half open doorway staring into the densely packed trees. Dozens of creatures probably call this place home like the turkeys I saw earlier. Maybe I should chill out and try doing the same.

Still, I feel on edge.

Get it together, I repeat to myself. Get it together. Get it together.

With the electric buzz of panic coursing through me, I flip the deadbolt on the door and walk through the house to be sure all the windows are locked. Nothing can get in unless I let it. Nobody is here.

The house is not haunted.

Nobody is watching me.

My hands shake as I go through the cupboards in the kitchen in search of something to calm me down. I find a bottle of red wine, local like the coffee left for me, and uncork it with only a slight struggle.

Then, because I am absolutely not washing an actual wine glass tonight, I grab a jar I find at the back of the cupboard with the remnants of a label still on its face. Classy. At least if anyone *is* outside tapping on my windows, they might feel bad for me in my current rock-bottom state and put me out of my misery quickly.

Scritch scritch scritch.

Scritch scritch scritch.

I go back into the bedroom and check the window again, but not before taking the shiny five iron—a trophy I took to inconvenience Brent later—that leans against the wall beside my still packed suitcase. Beef has awakened, and he stares out the window. Dark pupils spill over into his normally yellow eyes, turning them into black voids absorbing all the light they can find.

"What do you see?"

He lets out a deep, heavy rumble of a growl, then opens his mouth to show teeth.

In the living room behind me, something crashes to the floor and shatters. I turn and find the fake hydrangeas and the jagged pieces of their vase scattered across the room. As I approach to clean it up, I notice soil among the sharp chunks of ceramic. Who puts fake flowers in dirt?

More importantly, how did they fall if both Beef and I were in the bedroom? Every possible entrance has been locked.

"Is there somebody in here?" I call, standing tall with my weapon at the ready.

Every room I check shows no signs of an intruder. All the closets are vacant except for the items stored inside. The bed barely has a dust bunny. I even check the cabinet under the sink, which contains only cleaning supplies.

With a belly full of wine and adrenaline and my hands clasped tightly around the five iron, I feel powerful enough to go outside. I flip on the front light as I step out onto the deck, though the glow doesn't reach very far. My eyes adjust to the darkness as I step out of the light's reach, then I make a left to circle the cabin. My boots crunch dried leaves from the past autumn, giving away my presence and ruining any chance I had at surprise.

"Who's out here?" I demand.

In this moment, I wish my voice weren't so feminine. I don't sound threatening. Nobody takes me seriously because I sound like the blue Powerpuff girl — thanks Brent for the comparison that will never die now.

"If you're a person, you're not funny," I say. Maybe someone will laugh in response to Bubbles' attempt at scaring them away. "If you leave now, I won't call the cops on you."

I won't call the cops at all. First of all, I'm not sure Bowen's Leg has a police department, and, second of all, what good would they do? Worst case they shoot some kid for being a minor pain in my ass. Best case, they find nothing and still waste everyone's time and tax dollars. I'll figure this out myself.

The new me will solve her problems instead of burying them and becoming complacent.

As I come around the back of the house, I shine my phone's flashlight into my bedroom window and see Beef staring out into nothing. I try and follow his eyes, which lead into the dark, open yard behind the house towards the barn.

Confident from the alcohol, I wander away from the house a bit until my light catches reflective eyes, then I process the outline of a blurred figure. It's human sized — definitely not another turkey — though I can't make out any of its features or limbs, only a shapeless form rushing into the forest.

My heart spasms in my chest. What the fuck?

"Hey!" I yell, still unthreatening. "Get back here."

I stick my phone in my pocket and chase the figure with the golf club held like a bat poised to hit a grand slam, but I lose them among the trees I don't dare enter myself. Not in the dark. Not alone. Not when I know there's someone here.

My breath comes ragged by the time I reach the cabin and slam the door behind me. I don't know what I just saw. Could it have been a person? It had to have been.

Logic fails me, and my mind nags at me to go clean up the ceramic that broke and then settle in with Evie's journal. If nothing else, trying to solve the mystery of what she did and where she went might distract me from the ghosts inside my head. Best case, maybe I'll find an answer to at least a few of the questions I have after what I just saw.

Inside, though, the gray and green vase with fake blue and purple hydrangeas sits intact atop the small table it had been on earlier. There is no trace of dirt or broken ceramic anywhere. I pull the flowers out of the vase and look inside. No dirt, only a styrofoam insert to keep the flowers in perfect position.

What the hell?

CHAPTER

FIVE

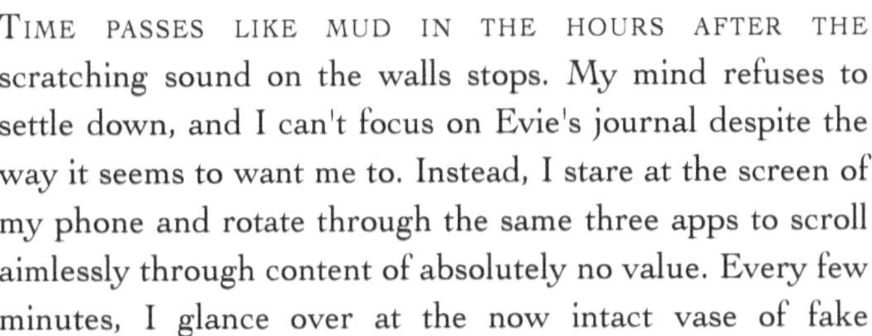

TIME PASSES LIKE MUD IN THE HOURS AFTER THE scratching sound on the walls stops. My mind refuses to settle down, and I can't focus on Evie's journal despite the way it seems to want me to. Instead, I stare at the screen of my phone and rotate through the same three apps to scroll aimlessly through content of absolutely no value. Every few minutes, I glance over at the now intact vase of fake flowers.

I should be doing something else.

Even though I vaguely remember a few short videos of cute cats, some easy recipes, and people lip syncing to seven seconds of the same three audio clips, I couldn't tell you any of the exact details. The content enters my brain with no intention of staying, yet the minutes pass.

The weight of Evie's journal on my lap nags at me to pick it up and explore the secrets its pages hold, and I want to, but my arms don't respond to signals to reach for the book. The phone holds me hostage and I keep scrolling until finally the LOW BATTERY warning appears on the face of the screen. It forces me to set the device down and plug it in, leaving me without an excuse to ignore the journal for any longer.

I open the cover and flip past the page declaring Evie's ownership of the journal and its contents.

At first, Evie writes about the all consuming grief that devours a person after a the shock of losing someone wears off. Someone she'd been close to, a woman named Betty, died. Rather, according to Evie's account, someone killed Betty, and Evie firmly planted herself in the anger stage of grieving.

He says he doesn't know what happened to her, that he came home and her car was gone. She was gone. I don't know why people want so badly to believe he didn't have anything to do with it, because his story implies she simply left him. But I know. I know he killed her. I know he found a way to make it look like she left on her own.

Nobody believes me when I tell them what really happened. They don't want Betty's killer to be someone they know. Someone they trust. If Benjamin did kill her—and I know he did—it means they've golfed with a murderer, sat beside one at dinner, shook hands and broke bread with one at church.

If I know anything about this town, it's that people will stand by him. They'll believe his story, because admitting he's a killer means admitting their initial judgment of him was wrong.

A chill runs through me, and my eyes wander to the corner of the room where walls meet ceiling. I stare off into that space for a while, considering Evie's words and how I too have a man similar to Benjamin in my life. Had. The kind people like. The kind whose mistakes are forgiven, simply so those in association with the offender don't look bad themselves.

I want to figure out where Evie went. What happened to her. She deserves to be searched for, and maybe even to be found. Someone needs to tell her story, if for no other reason than to take it back from a man she might've killed, a man who might not have been innocent himself.

If I choose to believe the rumors Elise shared with me, what does that mean?

Is she what I thought I saw in the woods tonight? Is she the one haunting this house?

The first entry ends with more damning of Benjamin, and I skim long paragraphs where the words had been stabbed into the page rather than written. Her anger comes off the page like heat from a stove.

He deserves worse than death. He deserves an eternity of hellfire and misery, and I'll find a way to give that to him in life. He can try and kill me too, if he wants, and I'll be with him until he goes mad and begs me to let him rest.

Those last lines linger with me into the night long after I've set the journal in the drawer in the bedside table. I lie awake thinking about what she meant. Obviously she wanted this guy dead when she wrote those words. Was it only the grief talking, or could she really have found the strength to tear his life apart? I think about her in the thick minutes before I fade into sleep.

I DECIDE WHEN I WAKE UP THAT I NEED TWO THINGS: A distraction from what I read last night, and a plant to spruce up the house a little bit and make it feel more like my own. A part of me regrets that I didn't take anything but the cat and what clothes I could fit in a suitcase—the clothes Brent hadn't bought for me, of course—and the five iron I stole from his set of clubs just to inconvenience him.

Nothing back in Wisconsin really felt like mine anyway. Everything matched his style, this crisp, modern aesthetic that felt as fake as the smile he wore when taking prospective customers out on the green or out to expensive dinners before closing a deal. He had so much expensive shit to keep up appearances. Nautical themed stuff—though he'd never been in a kayak, let alone a yacht—top tier golf clubs, modern art, fake plants because he didn't like the idea of dirt inside the house. He barely tolerated the cat.

None of his shit would match the woodsy, rustic cabin plucked straight from a Hallmark holiday special.

You know what? Fuck Brent. I'm going to get two plants.

Before I go for plants, I stop at the tiny grocery store to pick up a few staples for the kitchen so I can attempt to get in a better habit of feeding myself. Things like pasta, frozen meals, oatmeal, and, of course, more coffee. Oh, and two bottles of red wine from the surprisingly well-stocked liquor section.

As I stand in the short line for checkout, I think about the vase of flowers, the contents of Evie's journal, and the blur of a figure I saw in the woods last night and the way I've felt eyes on my back since arriving. In the time since the encounter, my mind has warped the image until I want to believe I saw a cat. Not a person. Not a ghost. A cat is a perfectly good explanation. Maybe Roger had one and nobody knew about it, so it took to the woods to survive. It wouldn't be unreasonable to believe it would come home at the first sign of life. Why hunt and fight to stay alive when there's a perfectly good human to give you food? That's Beef's philosophy, at least.

The cat explanation, however, does not explain the scratching I heard inside the cabin. It started in the bedroom and bathroom, and only me and Beef were inside. If he'd been awake, I'd blame him. He would raise hell if he sensed another cat on his turf. But I saw him sleeping, and he doesn't move fast enough to trick me like that.

Besides, even if I could explain the scratching, I can't explain the vase. It was broken. There was dirt scattered on the floor. Then, it was fixed and the only thing inside was styrofoam.

I turn all the possibilities over and over in my head. I will figure this out, even if I don't like where my mind goes.

For the rest of my time in the grocery store and most of the drive to the farm and garden store, I remain in a fog. I have to stop and let an old pickup pass before I make the left into the store's parking lot, and I notice it's the first hint of traffic I've seen since I arrived. Bowen's Leg hasn't been thriving in a long time, and I wonder how long before it fades completely. Will it take me with it when it goes? Would that really be so bad?

My car stutters to a stop when I park, and something metallic creaks underneath when I close the door behind me. I ignore it and head for the greenhouse built on one side of the store. I make for a rack of houseplants and stand in front of it with my hands on my hips as I attempt to decide which two to take home with me.

There's cacti and succulents, pothos, ivy, ferns. So many options. Though I want them all, I pick a round, spiky cactus with a little orange flower off center on the top, and then hover my hand over a leafy plant in a blue ceramic pot.

I stop for a moment and consider looking for one in a plastic pot. It would be tragic to lose a real plant. Surely they couldn't survive what the fake flowers went through last night. Assuming that actually happened.

"Come back to check the status of dirt on my face?" A familiar voice comes from behind me.

I turn, cactus in hand, to find Jonah in his green vest and a new name tag with his name written in lowercase letters this time.

"Oh, you came for plants."

"I did." I lift the cactus like a toast. "Come for plants, I mean."

Why didn't I think about the possibility of running into him again? I should have come prepared. Now, I feel off balance because I don't know what to do now that we've established some sort of rapport as numbers in each other's phones. How do I keep making progress in this friendship?

"I didn't take much with me," I say. "I thought it'd be nice to leave my mark on the place I'm staying, since every-thing in there belongs to the previous owner and is prob-ably haunted."

"Well." He ignores the part about shit being haunted, and I appreciate that. "Are you looking for suggestions or do you know what you want?"

What the fuck? Did he just ask if I needed help rather than jumping straight to mansplaining plants to me? Wow.

"I am fully committed to this cactus. I would die for her honestly," I steal Tanner's line from the diner, enjoying the dramatic flair of the declaration. "But I'm open to ideas for the second." Sometime between taking the cactus off the shelf in its rustic metal pail, I decided it is a she and her name is Margaret. I don't share that with Jonah. "I don't want to spend a lot."

He asks what my skill level with plants is, and I wave my free hand in a passive gesture that says *medium*.

"Try this," he says, picking up a spider plant in a terra cotta pot. "Pretty low key, and it'll grow babies if you care for it right, which means more plants for your place."

"Perfect." I try and sound less enthusiastic, and therefore much cooler, than I am. The plant truly is perfect and I'll get more for the exciting price of love and attention.

"If you've named your cactus, you should name this one after me so you always know who helped you connect with it."

I blink, unsure if I told him I named the cactus and totally forgot about it. Otherwise, we're just on the same plant-naming wavelength.

"There is an exactly zero percent chance of me doing that. Thanks, though."

He grins like he knew I'd decline the suggestion to give my plant his name, and I wonder if he ever frowns. The curved lines on either side of his mouth suggest otherwise.

This has to be a work persona. No one can be this pleasant all the time, especially not in retail.

For some reason, though, I don't want to imagine that he might be hiding something—that maybe he's some kind of psychopath when he isn't here being friendly as hell. The thought dies quickly. I want to remain delusional if it means I know one person who isn't absolutely fucking miserable.

"We should hang out sometime," he says. "When you get sick of hanging out with the ghosts in your house."

"Oh, I'm already sick of them. Let me know when you've got a day off."

And, just like that, I definitely made my first friend.

CHAPTER

SIX

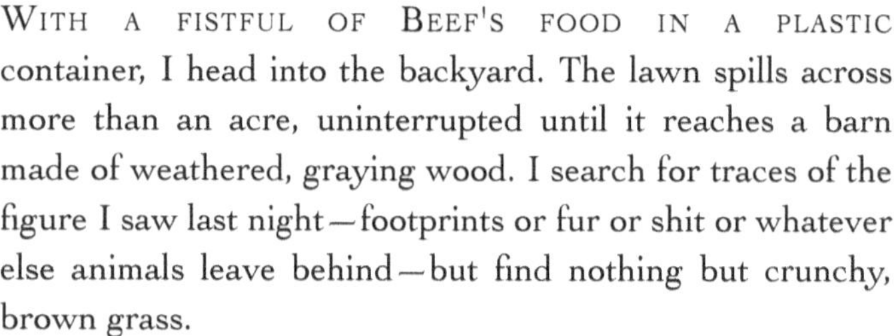

With a fistful of Beef's food in a plastic container, I head into the backyard. The lawn spills across more than an acre, uninterrupted until it reaches a barn made of weathered, graying wood. I search for traces of the figure I saw last night—footprints or fur or shit or whatever else animals leave behind—but find nothing but crunchy, brown grass.

The spot where I saw the apparition sits at the edge of the treeline. I stand there, at the edge of the forest and the eerie silence crescendos into the sounds of life. Acorns and branches falling from trees, sticks breaking under the small creatures that forage on the ground, and rustling of leaves and brush from those same animals. Somewhere far off in the distance, the faintest whoosh of a car goes by, as out of place as me. Whatever lives out here, it's more woods than human now. It's got nature braided into its soul, and even if we pulled them out, the ghosts would still be tangled in roots and vines.

The thought of ghosts is not welcome, yet it plants itself firmly in my head. It would be an explanation, albeit one I do not want to accept.

I make a mental check of how tired I feel and prepare to accept that I imagined everything. The animal, the scratching, the blurred silhouette. Nobody, least of all me, would be surprised if I were making shit up in my current state of exhaustion. Two decent nights of sleep have done nothing to remedy the twitch in my eye or the biting pain in my temples. All I want is more sleep, but sleep brings dreams and dreams bring things I don't want to think about.

Keep going, I tell myself. Eventually, I'll reach where I need to be and then I can rest. Close my eyes. Dream.

Eventually feels a long way away.

I make that *pspsps* sound cats respond to, hoping to see a pair of pointy ears emerge from the barn or the woods. Somewhere over the course of the day, I decided what I saw definitely was a cat combined with a trick of the light. Someone must have fed it and it got used to being an almost pet, as most domesticated cats tend to be. Poor thing must be hungry.

"Kitty. Come here, buddy. I've got food," I call.

The dry pellets bounce against the plastic when I shake the container. If Beef were the cat I'm after right now, he'd be halfway up my leg by now. I wince a little thinking about the one time he scaled me like a tree, claws dug into my flesh through my jeans and gravity tugging his full weight down against my punctured skin.

Nothing comes to the sound of food this time, so I keep moving toward the barn. It somehow looks better and worse from up close. Structurally sturdier than I initially thought, though the roof bows inward towards the ground and the walls lean so slightly to the side, Some of the boards have grown warped and decayed and desperately in need of a coat of paint at the very least. It'll stand for a few more years, but it's fate looms ever present in its future. Soon it will collapse. Soon the woods will weave their way into its remains until they take over.

The front door is already most of the way open and I shudder at the thought of something—someone—living in here without me knowing. Aside from dirt and some leaves blown in from outside, the barn is immaculate like the house. It has two stalls that appear to have never had animals living in them, but two are occupied with machines. A riding lawnmower sits in one, the red metal faded from the dust collected in its disuse, but the machine is otherwise in perfect condition. The other stall has a vintage car backed in carefully and covered with a tarp. I don't look beneath the tight-fitted blue cover, but I assume the car looks as good as the lawnmower. Or, maybe it's full of mice.

Not removing the cover seems like a fine idea, at least for now.

It makes me sad seeing these things someone might have treasured now abandoned and collecting dust until someone can be bothered to sell them. I get a pang of something in my chest. What did Roger hope would happen to his belongings when he died? Did he know his children wouldn't come, and that a stranger would occupy his home?

The thought of what would happen to Beef was the only thing that kept me alive over the last few months, even before the divorce. Brent would've dumped the cat back in the shelter, at best, or abandoned him somewhere to fend for himself. I wasn't about to let that happen.

God, there were so many days I came so close to giving up. It would've been easy, but I never went through with it because the cat needed me. He was the only thing left to leave behind, and I wouldn't.

I shake the container of kibble again and look around for signs of something living in the barn. If I look hard enough, I'll find a nest in the corner of one of the stalls, in the rafters, somewhere.

The distinct scent of smoke reaches me.

Was something burning?

I search for a flame, or even a pile of ashes to indicate the presence of a fire long extinguished.

Still nothing.

"Here, kitty," I call again. "It's okay. I won't hurt you."

A tiny sound comes from one side of the barn, but I can't pinpoint the exact location. Quietly, I tiptoe closer.

The sound comes again, like the creaking of a loose board or old hinges on a swinging door. A kitten maybe? A little orphaned creature? I barely have the resources to care for myself and Beef, let alone another hungry belly. Yet I already know that, whatever it is, I'll find a way to give it what it needs.

I fixate on what could be in here, and my mind goes to a dark place. The ideas that bloom ache in my chest, the sharp edges of panic and helplessness I've grown accustomed to. The unwelcome thoughts bombard me with their violence, their gore, their misery and pain. No normal person would think like this.

I can have a panic attack in the most crowded room without anyone noticing my distress. I've mastered it. It is the one thing I have control over.

Yet now, alone in this barn, I want to let the anxiety that comes with my intrusive thoughts out into the mildewy air where it will dissipate and vanish into nothing. I want to cry.

The flashlight on my phone fills the dark corners of the

barn and the beam lands in vacant places. Between a metal toolbox and the wall, I find cobwebs. The empty place behind rakes and brooms leaned against the wall contains only dust.

The small sound returns and I feel the presence of something. A chill goes down my spine as I realize something is really here with me. I am not alone. The unfamiliar open space of the barn is more unsettling than the darkness last night. My instincts tell me to run but my stubbornness forces me to stay.

"Hello?"

There could be a person here, watching me. Some twisted soul could be hovering just out of sight, fucking with me for the fun of it, and I wouldn't be surprised. Two decades of the chemical imbalance in my brain presenting all the worst case scenarios has prepared me for this. If there's a murderer lurking, they won't have the element of surprise thanks to my anxiety working overtime.

The walls of the barn seem to shrink around me, and I turn on my heels to check behind me.

Nothing.

There is nothing here. I'm psyching myself out because I'm not used to being alone. My mind is playing tricks on me.

I spent so long battling invisible monsters that they started to feel like the real ones. They should be half a country away by now, though I've never been one to leave things behind. They've caught up to me here and have to make up for days of lost torment.

That has to be all this is.

Reflex makes me shake the container again, and the squeaking sound returns from somewhere behind me. I keep searching just in case. My light shines in every nook I can find, and nothing turns up. The sound is made up. This is all in my head.

"There's nothing here," I say to no one.

I am alone.

I am alone.

I repeat the words slowly to myself. Over and over until I can't get the taste of them out of my mouth.

I am alone.

The barn door groans as I slide it shut behind me, and I double-check to be sure to fix the latch before I leave so nothing new can take up residence in there. Ahead, the lawn sprawls towards the cabin, pale brown uninterrupted by shadows. The faint outline of Beef takes shape in the back facing window of the bedroom.

I am alone.

CHAPTER
SEVEN

WHEN I GET BACK INSIDE, I FIND BEEF LOOKING AT MY plants with the expression of a spoiled kid who opened a present to find a new pair of socks. He narrows his yellow eyes, displeased that the things I've chosen to bring into our new home are not something he can eat. Of all his terrible qualities, he doesn't mess with plants like some other cats. He prefers cheese, specifically provolone. Once, a neighbor in Madison brought him some fresh catnip and he left it discarded and wilted on the tile floor of the kitchen.

He meows, a sound closer to a raspy croak than anything that should come from a cat, and I add a handful of food to his bowl by the fridge.

I put the cactus in the bedroom on the nightstand next to the bed, then decide to set the spider plant on the windowsill above the kitchen sink. It makes the place feel a bit more like home now that I've left a small mark of my own.

With the plants situated and the barn thoroughly investigated, I'm at a loss for what to do. Before, my to do list never ended. I worked my office job with Elise nine hours a day doing mundane tasks worth no real developmental value, then I came home to switch into housewife mode. Brent expected me to keep the house how he liked it because my job was "easier" or something like that.

He left his laundry in piles and I trailed behind to collect it, wash it, fold it, iron it. He worked long hours and made the money that bought us our expensive house, so I needed to pull my weight through cooking and cleaning.

As it turns out, those long hours were a hybrid of working and fucking other women, and I'm just a goddamn sucker.

This house is already tidy, and I don't have enough dirty clothes to justify doing a load of laundry. What do I even enjoy doing? At some point, I had hobbies and interests. What were they? Did I stop doing anything I actually enjoyed when I left the stable and tried doing "normal teenage girl things."

I pace the house and text Elise, stopping occasionally to linger at the bookshelves full of mysteries and thrillers—all with age worn covers and cracks in their spines. So Roger, or maybe Evie, was quite the reader.

I type a message and send it.

Marisa:
It's so quiet here. It's creepy.

Elise doesn't need to know about the sounds I thought I heard or the figure I thought I saw.

While I wait for her response, I pick the most worn out book on the shelf and hold it in both hands as I examine the cover. The title and author don't stand out to me, but a line of text at the top compares it to one of the most popular supernatural thrillers.

> **Elise:**
> You'll get used to it. Are you settling in okay? The office is horrible without you.

Elise replies, text riddled with emojis. Specifically the one with X's for eyes to signify having died.

On the first page after the book's cover, I find a note written in terrible handwriting.

For Evie. Maybe one day you'll pick up an interest in nicer books. Love, Roger.

After the note, Roger drew a winking smiley face. Something about it makes me think he either didn't know or didn't believe Evie was suspected of murder. And I find it hard to believe he didn't know the rumors.

> **Marisa:**
> Did Roger believe the rumors about Evie?

> **Elise:**
> I don't know. When people came to the house with questions, he'd send them away. Some people believe that makes him a suspect in her disappearance, or an accomplice in whatever she did. I don't know.

> **Marisa:**
> I read some of her journal. She talked a lot about revenge for killing her friend.

Elise:
Betty was Evie's first love, not her friend.
They were together, I guess had to hide it,
and eventually they both married men.
Betty's fate is as unknown as Evie's, except
Evie ran around town telling everyone
Benjamin killed his wife.

Marisa:
Got it.

Elise:
Yeah, it's a whole thing.

Marisa:
What do you think about the rumors?

Elise:
At this point, it's enough of a local legend
that there's so many different versions that
anyone can choose one to believe.

I gotta get back to work, but let me know
what you find in the journal.

I set the book back on the shelf and digest the conversation. The thing that sticks with me most is how Roger might've known what she did and loved her despite it. It makes me wonder how long they were married and what they did to preserve what they had. Loneliness builds an ache in my chest, because Brent was supposed to be a happily ever after for me.

All I can think to do is pick up Evie's journal and keep reading, so I sit cross-legged with it at the end of the couch. Beef sidles up to me and leans half his weight on my thigh, then stares up at me to be pet. His purring radiates through my bones, comforting me like he always does when I need it most.

"This sucks, buddy," I say to the cat.

Beef slowly blinks, then gets more comfortable against me as I scratch his favorite spot between his ears.

I wish I could erase everything from before I came here. I want to forget. Everything reminds me of something I don't want to hold on to anymore.

Evie's anger has settled in most of what I read today. She writes short entries about nothing interesting. She writes about her day, though I can't determine how old she is or when all of this takes place. I imagine the person writing this as a woman about my age, maybe a few years older, and in a similarly desperate mental state. Probably, worse, but I don't feel the need to compare traumas with a woman who could be long dead. Call that self-improvement.

A vibration startles me as my phone comes to life in my pocket.

At first, I assume it's another text from Elise, but it keeps vibrating and the screen shows an incoming call from the thumbs down emoji. My heart leaps into my throat. What the hell does he want? I press the red decline button and wait to see if a voicemail comes in.

The device trembles in my shaking hands, a mix of anger and anxiety, until I set it down. No message. No follow up text.

My heart pounds. Beef complains because I've stopped petting him, and he pulls my hand back to his head with his paw. His soft fur, thick and warm, eases the feeling of my entire body short circuiting.

He didn't mean to call me. It was an accident. A reflex from years of being the first person he'd contact. Someone else was meant to be on the other end of that call. Not me. He doesn't want me anymore. I don't want him.

I grind my teeth and remind myself that I left because he wanted me to go. He doesn't get to occupy space in my head forever. Eventually he'll fade. Eventually, and only if he doesn't make shit like this a habit.

There's that word again. *Eventually.* It's starting to become a word I hate.

Even though I got out alive, I already know I was wrong about leaving being the hardest part.

For a while, I sit there with Beef. I focus hard on my breathing until I bring myself back under control.

The house grows silent around me except for the sound of Beef's purring and tiny, squeaking snores. He's passed out cold against me, so I pick up the journal again.

> *This town may not seem like much, but beneath the surface*
> *there are people who have seen and done sinister things.*
> *Benjamin thinks he got away with what he did, but I won't*
> *allow it. He won't get a quick punishment. When I'm done,*
> *he'll wish I'd simply put a bullet between his eyes.*
> *No, I will savor the end of him.*
> *Then, I'll leave him to the fire, because fire cleanses*
> *everything.*

In the quiet, a distant banging noise stands out among the whistling of the wind. It sounds like fists on a door demanding to be let in. The pounding is close, but not on the door of this house.

With a clap, I slam the journal shut and tuck it under a pillow as though opening it summoned Evie's wrath. Beef wakes and glares at me.

"What's out there?" I ask.

Surrounded by trees, I don't know what anyone could be knocking on right now other than either the front or back doors. The wind would drown out the sound before it reached me if it were coming from the barn.

The feeling of not being alone returns. As much as I want to recede into the cushions of the couch and forget about curses and revenge, I rise to be sure I locked the front door.

CHAPTER

EIGHT

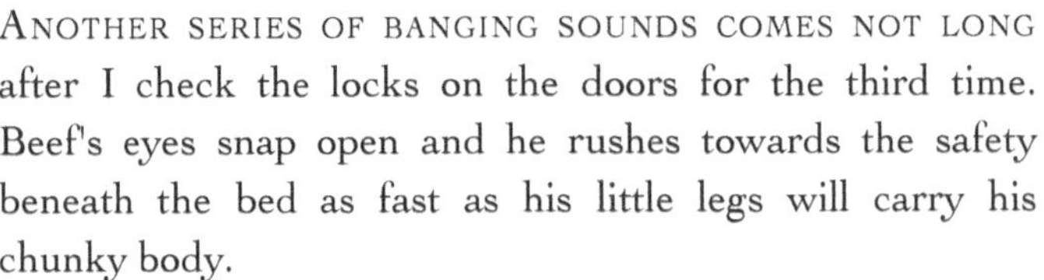

Another series of banging sounds comes not long after I check the locks on the doors for the third time. Beef's eyes snap open and he rushes towards the safety beneath the bed as fast as his little legs will carry his chunky body.

I expected there to be sounds when I moved to the woods, but this is getting out of hand. Scratches on the walls, and now pounding on some surface in the yard. I expected the slow hooting of owls, the rustling of small creatures in the brush, maybe the droning of insects when the weather warmed.

I didn't expect to be this afraid.

The sun hasn't set yet, and it casts the yard in a hazy, golden glow, so I pick up the five iron leaned against the wall by the door. The stubborn part of me—or perhaps it's the part without an ounce of self preservation—pushes me

49

toward the door to go out there and find whoever has been messing with me since I arrived.

The banging hasn't stopped, and going outside seems like a terrible idea to the logical part of me, but I have to know. The old Marisa wouldn't go outside. She'd let Brent handle it.

The new Marisa handles her own problems.

Besides, I have a weapon.

The noise stops when I shut the door behind me, and I scan the area for signs of something out of place. This shit is getting real old, real fast, and I need to find whoever's doing this and get them to leave me alone.

Even though I scoured it and found nothing earlier, I make for the barn. The front door I know I latched is still closed like I left it. My fingers tighten around the golf club's handle as I go back into the place I deemed safe mere hours ago.

"Hello? Is there anyone in here? Do you need help?" I ask into the darkness.

Something bangs against the wall and I startle. The sliding doors clatter on their track. Footsteps follow, too heavy to belong to a person.

The pounding doesn't come again though. Thankfully.

At the other end of the barn, something grunts. I check around me for signs of someone having been here, but the barn holds nothing I didn't see earlier. If it does, the darkness envelops it.

I send a quick text to Elise to let her know to, I don't know, call the cops if she doesn't hear from me again within the next hour. She's the only one who will know to send help if the feeling in my gut isn't lying to me and there's really danger here.

The thought sends a buzz up my spine, but I keep moving until I reach the place where the grunting came from. Another heavy exhale fills the otherwise silent building.

Finally, I lay eyes upon the source of the noise, and I stumble back and catch myself on the half wall of an empty stall behind me.

"What the fuck?" I breathe.

The five iron clatters to the floor as I try to comprehend the presence before me. There is no way this is real. It can't be possible.

I checked every corner of this place, and there wasn't a single sign of life. A mouse or a bird could have slipped past my searching eyes. Maybe even a cat or dog could have gone unseen.

Not this.

There is no way I could have missed this.

A horse—a fucking full sized, whole entire horse— stares back at me as if I've deeply offended it by disturbing it.

How?

How could someone have snuck into my yard with a horse, left it in the barn, and gotten away without my noticing? And why would anyone go to the trouble?

Against my better judgement, I reach for the animal's muzzle, half hoping I've hallucinated the entire thing. My fingers meet velvety, soft skin.

My mind races and grabs at possible next actions. I could call the police and tell them someone did the opposite of kidnapping a horse, but that sounds impossible. They wouldn't believe me.

Marisa:
Elise. Did your uncle have a horse?

Because there's a horse here and I have no
fucking clue where it came from.

I'm not messing around.

I pick up the golf club, then rummage through all the stuff in the barn in hopes of finding something to help in this situation, though I don't actually know what I need right now. Buckets? Ropes? Grain for the horse? Everything I remember from my childhood days spent around horses has evaporated.

What do I do?

The only thing remotely useful in the barn is a medium black bucket, which I can use to give the horse water for the night while I figure out what to do next.

That's one problem solved, I guess. Doesn't do anything about the fact that there is a horse in the barn though.

"What in the hell ..." I mutter.

The horse's ears perk up at the sound of my voice. It's been so long since I've been around one, I worry I won't know how to act. But now, bucket in hand, the knowledge built up over a decade spent in barns rushes back into my brain.

How shitty of someone to leave a thousand pound animal in someone else's barn. The horse must be as freaked out as I am.

I have nowhere to bring her. No way of transporting her even if I did have a place. Maybe Jonah knows someone. He does work at the farm store, he must know plenty of people with horses. I wonder if he'd help me.

First off, I wonder if he'd believe me if I explained this to him. I'll have to think of a good lie.

I'll deal with that later. Right now, I need to go fill this bucket so the horse has drinking water.

I check the water spigot on the backside of the barn, but nothing comes out. The water has probably been shut off for the colder months, so I make the trek back to the house knowing full well the walk back with a heavy bucket will be exhausting.

While the bucket fills in the sink and Beef stares at me with questions in his expression, I try and come up with a plan. I need grain and hay to feed her. I'll have to check the fence to be sure none of it has fallen so she can go out and run. Horses cost money, lots of it, and that's assuming they're healthy. This one could be sick or injured and then what?

I better check.

Before I go, I glance at the picture on the wall of Evie and her horse. The animal in the picture bears a striking resemblance to the one currently residing in the barn, but it can't be the same one. The horse was full grown in 1993. It would have died years ago.

The two creatures look so alike, down to the white spots on their faces against an inky, black coat.

I haul the bucket out of the sink and groan. The muscles in my arms strain to hold the full bucket. I was so much stronger as a twelve year old. Hauling buckets was never this hard. Was it?

The journey across the yard takes forever, and I splash water down the front of me with each step.

Back in the barn and without a hook to hang it from, I set the bucket in front of her on the ground in the stall. It's not ideal, but at least she'll have water for the night.

While she's distracted and splashing her nose in the water, I check her for injuries. At first glance, she looks fine. A little thin, but still not the kind of animal someone would dump. Her coat is smooth and shiny, black like the night sky. The black covers her entire body except a thin white marking on her face, slightly off center, and a white "sock" on her front right foot.

The similarities between this horse and the one in the photo shatter my composure.

It's too eerie, too impossible. Elise hasn't responded, but I already think I know what she'll say. Roger didn't have a horse here. This has to be some kind of mystery for me to solve on my own. A test from the universe.

It has to have something to do with me looking into Evie's disappearance and foolishly thinking I can solve it. Why else would a carbon copy of her horse have appeared here? Something doesn't want me trying to find out what happened to Evie and Benjamin that caused this house to be the setting of a local legend.

I ignore the fact that all of these thoughts are completely unreasonable, and at the very least there have to be some differences between the horse here and the one in the photo.

My imagination goes wild.

Fuck, I need therapy. Not because of the horse. I should have done it years ago, back when I might've been able to afford it. I don't have a chance at it now. Especially not now.

"Okay, horse. I'm gonna, I don't know, go back inside. I'll check on you in the morning." If you're still here, I think.

The animal looks at me with dark, glistening eyes, trusting me more than I deserve. If only she knew how much of a disaster I am.

I can't keep her. I can't.

Elise:
Uncle Roger didn't have a horse when he died.

How did it get there?

Marisa?

Marisa? Are you okay?

Marisa:
I don't know. Yes, I'm okay...

IT TAKES THREE HOURS AND TWO GLASSES OF WINE FOR the shock to wear off. When it does, it leaves me feeling hollowed out and exhausted. Beef has returned to the couch from his place under my bed, and I sit beside him—careful not to move and disturb his rest.

I don't know how long I stare at the entry for Asshat—I mean, Jonah—in my contacts. He's first in the list, followed by Dad's number, then Elise. The thumbs down emoji lingers at the bottom where it belongs. I leave it there in case he calls again like he did earlier. Eventually I'll forget the sequence of numbers belonging to him, and I don't want to risk answering.

Deleting him would be better. Blocking his number and forgetting about him until he is no more than a bitter taste in the back of my mouth. I don't know why I can't go through with it.

Maybe I can't get rid of him yet because I keep running through the perfect lines, practicing what I'll say if he calls again. Each word is picked with the intention of causing harm. I want him to feel like shit. I want him to feel the way I do.

God, I can't think about Brent right now.

There is a horse in the barn and I don't know what to do.

And I'm thinking about my stupid ex-husband who doesn't matter anymore.

With a thumb, I tap Jonah's contact and hover over the option to send a message.

I can't think of a good way to explain this in only a few words without it sounding like a joke or something, and Jonah has no reason to believe I wouldn't do that.

The first few messages I type up, I delete before sending. If I really want to tell him what happened, I'll end up writing a huge paragraph. Talking it out would be the best way to do this, but I can't just call him. I honor the Millennial slash Gen-Z code of ethics that includes never calling someone on the phone without asking if it's okay first.

> **Marisa:**
> Hey, it's Marisa. Do you have a minute?

I hit send fast enough that I don't have time to second

guess myself. The message goes out, first sent, then delivered.

He replies quickly.

Asshat:
Sure. What's up?

Marisa:
Something weird happened. Do you think
we could video chat?

I hate asking. A little part of me hopes he doesn't want to so I can call it a day, but the rest of me knows I need him to say yes.

This time, it takes him longer to respond.

Crap. Fuck. I scared him. So much for making friends out here.

As easy as it would be to set the phone down and accept that he won't reply, I stare at the short string of texts and will him to start typing again.

"Please," I say to the phone. "I need help."

A pro of having been with Brent for so long is I know how to get to an almost comfortable numb while being made to feel like I'm crazy. If Jonah thinks that, it won't bother me. I'm used to it. That's how pros and cons work, right?

Asshat:
Okay, yeah. Sorry. Almost burned my grilled
cheese. Hit me up.

Oh. Okay.

I press the button to initiate a video call and, when my face fills the screen, I see how pale I am. Ghostly. Sick. For the first time in my life, I have defined cheekbones. It is not a good look.

"Hey!" Jonah still wears his green vest from work when

he answers his phone, and I can't believe I saw him just this morning when I went to buy plants. It feels like so much more time has passed.

"Hi." Beef pops his head up, having recognized I've started a video call. Somehow, the cat understands the concept of video calling and is obsessed with seeing his round face in the small magic rectangle.

He crawls up my stomach and sits down hard, turning to get a view of his corner of the screen. He sees himself, and is quite pleased. The cat's front paws jab into my abdomen like knives. Despite looking like cute little mittens, they feel sharp as hell when they hold up the rest of his weight.

"I'm sorry. He just … I don't know why he's like this." I nudge the cat off me, and he tumbles dramatically onto the empty cushion beside me.

Jonah waves me off—a *no problem* kind of gesture—with a triangle cut half of a sandwich in his free hand. It is a perfectly golden browned grilled cheese, and for a split second I am distracted by the pure sexiness of the skill this man possesses.

"What happened? Are you okay?"

"This is going to sound completely and absolutely batshit, okay? Promise me you'll let me finish before you hang up on me." It's a lot to ask of a stranger, really, but I ask it anyway because I don't have it in me to come up with a lie right now.

"Um. Okay." He takes a bite of his sandwich.

"So, I'm kind of housesitting for a bit, and the place I'm staying is set back in the woods. There's a barn out back with a little pasture for horses, but there's no animals. There's just an old car and lawnmower in the barn, right?"

He nods and sets the sandwich down, then his hand returns with one of those tiny pickles Brent's friends always served with hunks of cheese and meats on beautiful wood boards.

I tell Jonah how I heard the scratching last night and decided to follow it. How I saw a figure near the treeline and convinced myself it was a cat. He listens intently, crunching on gherkins while I go through the part where I searched the yard and barn today for traces of a person or animal and found nothing.

"Okay, so now for the weird shit. I latched the barn door shut. I know I did. I said the word aloud to myself, like stood there and said 'latched' to help me remember. And it was still latched when I went out tonight after I heard this loud banging noise."

It appears Jonah has run out of snacks, because now he leans forward with his chin propped up on a closed fist. His dark hair sticks up like it did when we first met. "What made the noise? Did you find it this time?"

"Yeah, I did. It was a horse." No sense dancing around the truth. "An *entire* horse. Not a little pony or whatever. A horse. In the barn. Which was still closed tight from when I narrated myself latching the door. I have no idea where it came from or how anyone could bring it here without me noticing."

His eyes go wide and I don't know him well enough yet to read his expression, but I hope it isn't disbelief.

"Did ... um ... does someone board their horse there and the owner forgot to tell you?" he suggests.

"The owner's dead, and the barn was spotless. If a horse had been living there, there'd be shavings in the stalls and there'd be feed bins and stuff. There isn't any of that. Besides, I texted my friend who hooked me up with the place and she said the guy didn't have a horse or anything. She would have told me."

Jonah frowns and looks like he's putting something

together in his head. He glances up and to the right, contemplating what to say next.

"You're living in the Ouellette house, aren't you?"

I blink. "How did you guess?"

"Earlier you said something about your house being haunted. Now you're telling me a horse showed up out of nowhere."

"You don't believe me."

"No, I do. I promise I do. That place isn't … right."

I nod my head once in agreement, then bite my lip to stop it from trembling. If anyone asked why I felt like crying, I couldn't explain it. He believes me, and the concept is so foreign that all I can think to do is break down. That special pain at the back of my throat from years of training myself not to cry throbs, and I try to swallow it but it won't pass.

The walls seem to close in around me, and I have to breathe manually to keep control over myself.

Jonah's words remind me of Evie's journal, but I don't dare mention it to him.

Could the horse be a manifestation of whatever Evie did? Is it possible she cursed this place?

I clear my throat hard before I speak again.

"No. It's not." I say more to myself in response to the thought I had, rather than to Jonah's comment.

The horse felt like a real animal. I touched its muzzle and felt its hot breath on my hand. It isn't a ghost or apparition. It is a horse.

"Like, even if it doesn't have some kind of spiritual dark cloud hanging over it, it's not a safe place. People harassed Roger for years before he died. They wanted an explanation he wouldn't give, and he paid for it with whatever information Evie left him to die keeping."

Beef reaches forward to curl a paw around the phone

and draw it closer to him. It falls and startles him, but he doesn't dart off this time. Instead, he squeaks somewhere deep in his throat when the device smacks against his face.

"Anyway, I'm not sure what to do," I say when I lift the phone back up.

"If you want, I'll come by in the morning and look around with you. We can evaluate the situation together."

Without a better option, I agree to Jonah's idea. He'll help me figure this out. This will all end up okay, even if he implied the house is worse off than I initially thought as far as Evie's haunting goes.

At worst, he'll show up and prove all of this is in my head. Actually, maybe that's the best case scenario.

CHAPTER

TEN

*I walked the path to Benjamin today and found him where
I left him. It isn't much of a path, but I remember the things I
passed. First a plastic bag I tied to a tree, a broken down truck,
a tree with the trunk split into a U shape, then finally a circle
of the very spruce trees I clipped for the ritual. They're beautiful trees, perfect for burning when they dry up.*

*The man has already begun losing his mind to a pain
induced madness. He sits tied to a tall chunk of granite in the
center of the circle of spruces. No matter how hard he pulls, the
forest won't let him go. He belongs to it now. He belongs to
me now.*

*Eventually, his body will wither out here, then his soul will
remain in the ashes. No sleep, no peace.*

BEFORE THE SUN RISES, I READ A BIT OF EVIE'S
journal until I find a part about Benjamin. If I believe
what Evie wrote, she really did it. Really found a ritual to

62

perform and place a curse on him so he'll live in misery forever.

Reading her words gives me a crawling feeling, like a thousand spiders on my skin.

Jonah shows up first thing as promised, and carries a bag of grain on one shoulder. For the first time since we met, he doesn't wear the green vest over his shirt. Instead, he wears a dark colored flannel over a charcoal henley with the top two buttons undone. What I presume are his day-off jeans have the beginning of a tear in one knee. His dark hair is, as always, tousled.

Between when we talked last night and now, I've twisted myself into a knot of anxiety. If the horse is real—and I don't understand how it couldn't be—I have an animal to care for or rehome. On the off chance it's fake, there will be so much more for me to make sense of. At least with the former, I know what to do with horses. I don't know where to even start in dealing with some paranormal entity living in my barn in the shape of an animal I've always loved.

Meanwhile, he showed up prepared with a bag of grain so I don't have to go out again.

"The barn's back there," I say, pointing behind me with a thumb.

"Huh. I could've sworn I heard the barn burned down," he says. "Guess not."

"Oh. Weird."

"Yeah. 'Weird' about sums up everything related to this place. Some people wish the whole house would burn down."

We walk side by side until we reach the barn, where I slide open the door and lead him inside. At first, it's quiet—almost alarmingly so—and I click my tongue to let the horse know we're here. She expresses her disinterest by huffing out her lungs' capacity of air and shaking her head vigorously. Horses, man. They really are something.

"This is the horse. I have now known her for 13 hours." I leave out the part where she looks exactly like the horse in the photo with Evie, because I can't bring myself to accept it. He'll notice on his own. "I didn't name her in case she belongs to someone but ... but who loses a horse? Is horse kidnapping a thing?"

Oh shit, what if someone's framing me for horse kidnapping?

No, that's irrational, not to mention a lot of work.

Jonah doesn't reach for the horse's muzzle to pet her like most people would. He eyes her carefully and keeps his arms crossed tightly over his chest.

"Are you afraid of horses?" I ask.

"No. Of course not. I just don't want her to bite me with her gigantic teeth, which, I think, is perfectly reasonable."

"Sounds like a phobia to me." Horse bites do suck, but picking on him lightens my mood. Sorry, Jonah.

I show him where to set the bag of grain, thank him for thinking to bring it, then search for a dry bucket for the horse's feed. A smooth, metal bowl big enough for a large dog will have to work, because I don't find anything better despite Evie having horses in here decades ago. Roger probably got rid of them after she vanished.

The horse gets excited when she hears me pour the grain, and she gently kicks the inside of her stall to tell me to hurry up. Jonah backs up a little farther from where she sticks her head over the half wall with her lips curled up and teeth showing. Her head bobs enthusiastically and he holds up his hands in defense.

My instincts from being a kid in a barn kick in, and I open the stall door without fear and nudge the horse out of my space with an elbow. She moves, but nibbles my already limp ponytail.

"Hey, can you not?" I set the bowl down and retrieve my hair from her mouth. It hangs stringy and damp against my back. A wave of deja vu comes over me, like this is a memory and not reality.

She hits the back wall again with a hoof and I close the stall door and leave her to eat. The grain looks silly in a bowl meant for a dog, but it'll work for now. This whole situation will be fine. For now.

"Thank you for the grain," I say.

Jonah finally takes his eyes off the horse to meet my gaze, and he nods. "No problem."

We stand there together for a minute in silence and the scent of sawdust and ash while the horse eats.

"So, uh. Looks like it's a real horse," I say. "Not an apparition or anything like that."

I think about the blurred figure I saw the night before the horse showed up. It looked human, or at least that's what I remember now. A new version of the memory has settled in and I can't imagine what I saw as anything but human, even if I wanted so badly for it to be a cat or a raccoon. I know what I saw.

"Yup." He shifts on his feet. "A couple friends of mine have horses. They might be willing to take her, if you want."

"Won't they have questions about where she came from?"

"Probably, but they also know this house's reputation. Everyone in town does." An edge of bitterness lines his words.

"Is it really such a bad thing to have a local legend? It must bring in some tourism."

Jonah shakes his head.

"Not good tourism. There's a cult of people that come

here looking for a Stephen King story, and they go home and exaggerate everything about the case and the town on their blogs or whatever. They paint the town as some backwards, hillbilly haven, and so that's what people find when they search the internet for Bowen's Leg. They make the locals look like idiots."

"Oh." I don't know what to say, because I know I too view this place as an outsider.

"Sorry, that was kind of a rant. It's just that this is my home and it's a good town with good people. Maybe even some good stories. But it needs someone to give a shit about it. I want to help make it a community people want to live in, but if people keep coming in and telling the entire internet about the small town quirks we have — like the fight club a group of folks started in the Farm & Garden parking lot a few years back — it'll attract the wrong crowd."

"You're allowed to love where you're from."

He exhales. "Thanks."

Jonah turns to his phone and texts someone, presumably asking them if they can take a horse in. I stare off into space — there's a little mouse or bird nest up in the rafters above the stall — and ponder my next move. I'd planned to ask Jonah to help me solve Evie's mystery, but I've changed my mind for now.

Instead, I decide to lighten the mood.

"Can you elaborate on the fight club?"

"Do you have a blog you're going to post it on?"

"No. Besides, I'm from South Dakota so legally I can't make fun of anyone else's small towns."

He grins.

Internally, I pride myself on having made a joke.

"It's not much of a story. People would hang out at the Wobbly Leg until last call, then they'd somehow wander to the Farm & Garden store and get into fights. The big story was when someone went full wrestle mania and chucked a dude through the front window of the store."

"Excuse me? They what?"

"There's not much to do in the off season, plus the Emergency Room is right across the street. It's the ideal set up for an unofficial fight club. No ambulance ride if you get too beat, just have a buddy toss you in a wheel barrow and haul you over."

"You're lying. That doesn't happen."

"We have to chain up the wheel barrows now so people can't use them as a budget ambulance."

"No. No way."

His laughter turns into a slight squeaky wheeze.

"Tell me you made it up. You're messing with me," I demand.

"I promise you it's the truth." His voice carries humor and sincerity, and all traces of bitterness have vanished.

The fact that people have fights in the parking lot of the garden store still sits wrong with me.

"It's weird here, and I'm allowed to tell the absurd stories of my hometown because they're partially mine. I have no reason to make this up."

"Okay, fine." I decide to let him have this one, though I'm still not convinced. It makes sense why someone not from here would take that story and make an insensitive joke out of it. "So what is the off season here then?"

"The off season is winter, the latter half of fall, and the beginning of spring. All the tourists and people who summer here head back to their warmer climates. Somehow, there is even less going on here when it's cold. Not much to do but go ice fishing on the lakes, if they freeze enough, or snowshoe. The days are shorter. Not like Alaska short, but short enough that people get fighty with all the cold and gloom."

To myself, I wonder what the hell kind of place I moved to. Small towns make sense to me. I grew up in one, but this is nothing like that. This is almost too small. An hour from the closest Wal-Mart or Target, not a single recognizable fast food chain except the rival outdated Tim Hortons and Dunkin Donuts situated in opposing gas stations.

I suppose this is as good a place as any to redefine myself. If I fuck up, I can leave my little mark and disappear again to a new place where no one knows me.

"I don't understand it here," I admit. "Why is it called 'Bowen's Leg?'"

"Oh no, don't pronounce it like that. You already sound a bit midwestern, and giving 'Bowen's' two syllables is a surefire way to stand out."

"I do not sound midwestern."

"You do though. Have you heard yourself use a vowel? It's great."

I pinch my face into a scowl. "Okay well, at least I acknowledge the letter 'r.'"

"What letter?" He purposefully says the word like 'lettah', forcing the gentle hint of an accent that blankets his speech into something more aggressive. "You'll be fine here. People will just think you're Canadian or something."

I throw a thumbs up, and in that very instant I wonder when I became more socially aligned with my South Dakotan dad than any person my gender or age. A thumbs up. Help me. "Could be worse."

We both laugh. Him because maybe I'm funny, and me because I feel like an absolute dork for pulling the thumbs up card and need to laugh it off.

ELEVEN

JONAH'S PHONE BLEEPS AND BRINGS US BACK TO THE present moment.

"My friends can take the horse in a couple days, but they're willing to lend you some stuff for the time being. If that's okay with you."

I hadn't even noticed him send a text.

"Sure," I say. It would be better if they could come now and get her settled in, but I don't say that because it might make me seem ungrateful. No need to make things more difficult.

"They asked for a picture of her, if you don't mind."

I nod. "Yeah, that's fine. I was thinking of putting her out to run for a bit anyway, so you can get a good shot in a minute."

Jonah goes pale.

"It'll be quick, and I'm sure your phone has zoom. You will be fine."

Without another word, I head back to the barn to get the horse and find out how big a lie I told Jonah about him being fine when I let the animal run.

Since I don't have any of the correct tack to lead the horse out—I really wish Roger or whomever hadn't purged the barn of Evie's stuff—I spend longer than necessary searching the barn for something reliable enough to get the job done. When I find only a rope, I stand in front of the stall with an end in each hand and stare at the animal in hopes of it telling me how best to do this.

"Okay. Time to go outside." I show her the rope and let her smell it before I loop it around her neck. She allows it, only huffing once when I tug gently to encourage her to step out of the stall and into the wide hallway.

"That's good," I say as she moves along with me. "Just out to the field. Don't you want to stretch your legs?"

She diverts to the side, sticking her face in an open metal trash can presumably to look for treats. When the bucket has been properly inspected, she extracts her head wearing—I swear on Beef's life—a full pout. How could I have forgotten how weird horses are? The true dumbasses of the animal kingdom. Cats are properly feral, but easily contained. Horses though? Off the rails. Unproblematic frat boys with giant bodies and tiny walnut brains.

I tug gently on the makeshift lead to guide her towards the pasture again, and she follows politely until we reach the dead grass at the barn's threshold.

She rears up, pulling the rope from my hands, and bursts full speed into the enclosure. I worry she might jump the fence, but she only sprints and occasionally breaks to kick at the air.

Jonah stands back from the fence, face drained of color and eyes wide.

I shut the barn door before the horse comes back around, then walk over to stand beside him.

"She's lively, huh?" I say.

At one point, all four of the horse's feet are off the ground like she might take flight.

"You were right earlier. I am definitely afraid of horses."

I lightly pat his shoulder, feigning sympathy. "Your secret is safe with me."

"Thanks, but is the structural integrity of my skeleton safe with you too? I really don't want to be kicked."

"Yes. You'll be okay."

Friendship is weird. Especially since I didn't know Jonah three days ago, and now we're here watching this nutcase of a horse attempt to reach a high enough speed to leave the atmosphere.

"Hopefully she'll settle down in a minute so we can get some photos. I don't want to take up your whole day off."

"It's fine. I only had laundry on the to do list for today."

I walk up to the fence and lean my elbows on the top rail like a cowboy. Once Jonah works through what I imagine is some mental safety checklist, he joins me, folding his hands together in front of him.

"Um, do you want a drink or something?" I ask, not sure what to talk about now.

What do people talk about when there isn't a topic dropped right in their laps?

"That sounds pretty good."

"I don't have anything great, so don't get too excited." Got to set those expectations, for fear he expects a macchiato from a six hundred dollar espresso machine. "The horse needs to cool her jets anyway."

The chance to leave the horse to blow off her pent up energy gets Jonah moving, and he's two steps ahead of me before I even have a chance to push myself back off the fence.

The walk up to the house doesn't take very long, and neither does picking from my meager supply of beverages. He opts for a grapefruit seltzer water, while I pour the rest of this morning's coffee into a cup with ice cubes. It isn't half bad, despite the thick ring of grounds that'd been circling the bottom of the carafe.

Jonah glances around the cabin, eyes taking in every detail of the small space.

"I've never been in here before," he says. "It's not what I expected."

"What did you expect?"

He takes a sip of his seltzer and considers my question. "Lots of cobwebs, probably. I imagined it would be much dirtier, like a typical haunted house. Maybe there might be an ambiguous stain on a rug that could have been blood."

"So, you just assumed I was living like the bad guy in a slasher film? In some condemned house full of filth?"

He shrugs. "You're the one living in the haunted murder house, not me."

"It's free in exchange for keeping an eye on the place. Presumably so your best friends, the bloggers, don't trespass." I dump the rest of my coffee into the sink. "Besides, they hired a cleaner. It could've been what you described before they tidied the place up. I have no idea."

WHEN WE GO BACK OUTSIDE, THE HORSE IS NO LONGER attempting to take flight.

"I should try taking her picture while she's standing still, shouldn't I?" Jonah gestures toward the center of the pasture where the horse snuffles around in the still brown grass. She discarded the rope I looped around her neck at some point during the run. I make a mental note to look for it. Later, when she's back inside. I'd prefer not to be in the pasture with her.

"Yeah, not a bad idea."

He slowly pulls his phone from his pocket, so as to not startle the now calm animal. He turns the device sideways and fiddles with the focus before taking two pictures back to back.

He screws up his expression when the images pop up on the screen, then wipes the hem of his shirt on the circular lenses on the phone's phace.

"You good?" I ask.

"Yeah." He lifts the phone again and takes a few more pictures, mouth moving with indistinguishable grumbling and eyebrows becoming more and more furrowed with each artificial click of the shutter. "Do you see a smudge on this?"

I set my glass down on a flat part of the ground, then take the phone from his hand. At first glance, the lenses look fine, but I breathe a hot breath on them and wipe the fog away with my shirt too for good measure.

"I don't see anything." I give the phone back to him and return to my place against the fence.

"Weird. Everything is coming out wrong," he says. "I'm no professional photographer or anything, but I know what makes photos come out bad. I have good light and the shutter on this is normally fine, but look."

He holds the phone out again with one of the images open in the screen. Blurry doesn't begin to cover it. The horse's entire figure is shrouded in a dark cloud, like fog or smoke. The surroundings all look fine, with the exception of a sliver of the barn caught in the frame.

"What the fuck?" I mutter.

"Right? I don't know what's going on here."

I frown at the phone as I scroll through a couple more images, careful not to go so far back that I see something I'm not meant to. The thought stops my thumb mid swipe for a moment while I process the preemptive flood of embarrassment that comes with the idea of seeing *that* kind of photo.

"They're all like that," I say. Discomfort crawls up my body until it settles in my chest, tightening my ribs around my lungs until my breath feels shallow. I don't know how to describe what I see on the screen.

"Every single one."

I stand beside him and watch as he taps the screen to focus on the horse, who stands perfectly still except for the occasional flick of her tail. He holds the device with both hands to steady it, and uses the phone's side button to take the picture. It shows a preview for a split second before switching back to live mode.

Still blurry.

No, not blurry. Smudged. Almost similar to the figure I saw in the woods the other night.

"Let me try something." I remove my own phone from my pocket and use the front facing camera to take a photo with both me and the horse in the frame.

Just like with Jonah's shots, the image showed clear in the live view, but the dark smudges cover the horse in my picture too. My face is in focus, unaltered.

"What could cause this?" I ask.

He shakes his head. "Nothing good, and definitely not something natural."

Jonah looks at the horse for another minute before suggested we take a photo of Beef. Though neither of us admit we already know how the pictures will turn out, I'm certain it's a waste of our time. Still, we go inside and do it anyway, unsurprised when the images come back clear.

Beef grumbles at the presence of a stranger, and sits alert beside me on the couch while Jonah stands a safe distance away.

"Will your friends still take her, even if we don't have pictures?" I ask.

"I think so."

"Okay."

All of this is so strange. I wish Elise did tell me about the horse and I agreed to care for her, and I simply forgot until just now. It wouldn't feel good, but I've forgotten things before. It would give me a logical explanation to cling to. Instead, we have a horse that appeared out of thin air and has some cursed electromagnetic something-or-other preventing us from taking its picture.

"Can I say something?" Jonah asks, tentative.

"Sure."

"You shouldn't stay here. Whatever is happening, it's only going to get worse. You're not safe here."

"And do what? If the place is part of Evie Ouellette's curse, then this stuff will keep happening with or without me here. I may as well stay and see if I can figure it out. Close the case, so to speak."

Fuck. I didn't mean to tell him I was trying to find out what happened to Evie and reverse whatever she did to Benjamin. Up until now, I didn't realize how firmly I believe Evie did *something* bad. Something she might not have meant to do, but something with lasting consequences.

Jonah's eyes go wide.

I hold a hand up. "I don't have a blog, and I don't plan on starting one. I won't slander Bowen's Leg. I just think maybe it's time Evie's story gets a real ending."

He processes the information for a beat, then rubs his eyes wearily.

"You found something in here, didn't you?" he asks.

"I found Evie's journal. I keep falling asleep or, like, disassociating, so I haven't gotten far but she admitted she put a curse on some guy named Benjamin. Or killed him. Or both."

Saying the words aloud makes me feel both empowered and absolutely unhinged at the same time. If Jonah hadn't already told me about the town's longstanding belief that this house is haunted or cursed, I might not have said the exact words I did. I guess I'm really taking the case of What The Hell Did Evie Ouellette Even Do? I've unlocked a new eccentric young divorcee achievement, surely.

"I don't like this," he says. "We haven't known one another long, so I'm not really in a place to make big requests and I've already told you to move out of your place, but I'm going to. Will you promise me you'll be careful? Not just in this house, but in town. Don't talk about this too loudly, because there is a lot of ire directed at this particular plot of land."

"I can do that." I offer a hand to shake on the deal, and he takes it. "Also, I wouldn't hate getting out of here for a little while, if you have any ideas?"

Jonah must have been holding both lungs full of air along with the tension in his body, because at my request to go do something, he exhales hard and his body visibly relaxes.

"So, you want the grand tour of Bowen's Leg?"

CHAPTER
TWELVE

out to his car, which happens to be the horrifically orange
Subaru I saw the first time I went to the farm and garden
store. That first day, I already had a feeling the car
belonged to him. He has extreme Orange Car Energy, even
if I couldn't tell you what exactly that means.

Before we head off into whatever grand adventure he
has planned, we stop at the Oceanside Diner for more
coffee, because, after the last couple days, caffeine is all
that's keeping me upright.

Tanner, the girl from the first time I visited the diner,
stands behind the counter. She raises an eyebrow when I
walk in with Jonah, and I decide to ignore it even if it
makes me want to turn around. Should I not be here with
him? She's too young to have a history with him, unless …
yikes.

I hate anxiety and the irrational thoughts it plants in my head.

"Would you look at that! Two of my favorite customers," she says, smiling at us both.

I try and fail to relax my shoulders. Stop overthinking. Stop.

Jonah approaches the counter, unaware of my sudden tension. When he leans on the surface and starts talking to Tanner, I notice his height for the first time. His blend of goofy but quiet confidence makes him seem so tall, but across from Tanner, I realize he can't be more than five foot nine. The younger girl has a good three inches on him.

"Marisa—it's Marisa, right? I'm not good at names, sorry," Tanner begins.

I nod.

"Okay. Yay. I remembered." Her dull tone contradicts how she clasps her hands together happily. "You look real stressed. Sit down. Have something to eat. It'll help."

Jonah turns and looks at me, then gestures with a hand to one of the stools. "A quick snack can't hurt before we head out."

Without a good way out, I take a seat and order a small coffee and a side of bacon, though I don't really want it. Tanner is probably right that I need to eat.

The three of us talk while I eat and we drink our coffee, and it feels wholesome. I've missed interactions like this, though I hadn't noticed until now as I watch these new people in my life interact and actually include me in the conversation. After I begin nibbling on the slices of bacon, my muscles loosen and my stomach settles.

"What are you two up to today? You actually have a day off, Jonah?" Tanner asks.

"I'm taking Marisa around to see the sights," Jonah says.

"The sights." Tanner gives Jonah a look I can't decipher. "All, what, two of them? What are you going to do, go have a lobster dinner and look at the ocean?"

"How many of the items on the itinerary are lobster?" I ask.

Jonah makes a performance of pondering the idea. "First of all, lobster is for tourists." He holds up a finger. "That said, you should try it if you haven't already. Get it out of the way before the actual tourists get here and restaurants hike the prices."

"So your grand tour of Bowen's Leg is going to get lobster?" How many times can I say the word 'lobster' before it starts to sound wrong?

Tanner chuckles as she refills my coffee.

"There's also a lighthouse and a beach." Jonah lists each new thing by counting on the rest of his fingers. "An old paper mill. The wildlife preserve. A candy shop that makes their own saltwater taffy right in the window."

"Oh wow. This place is happening. A cultural epicenter."

"Truly," Tanner agrees.

We finish up at the diner and say goodbye to Tanner, then Jonah and I walk a little ways down the sidewalk to the end of the block. A low set window displays an old machine pulling and stretching pastel colored candy. An antique sign advertises "choose your mix" taffy for eight bucks a pound.

I watch the machine pull the taffy for a while and wonder if I would have eventually noticed it on my own.

"Do you want to go inside?" Jonah asks.

We go down a narrow flight of stairs into the candy shop, which, like the diner, has a local teenager behind the counter. He's lanky and leans forward with a book in one hand. He glances up but doesn't greet us.

Jonah offers a polite hello before taking me past a wall of classic candy to a long row of wooden barrels, each filled to the brim with individually wrapped pieces of taffy. They have labels atop each with flavors written in marker to match the color of the candies. The entire place smells like sugar, like the hand dipped chocolates arranged inside the glass display case along the counter.

"What's the best kind?" The sheer number of flavors overwhelms me. Where do I begin?

Jonah answers without a moment of hesitation. "Neapolitan. Hands down."

I look for the barrel marked neapolitan, then grab a clear plastic bag from a dispenser on the wall. Unable to visualize what a pound of taffy would be, I take two of each flavor—except bubblegum because that shit is nasty—and make for the counter after I drop two of Jonah's suggested flavor right at the top. According to the kid working the register, who reluctantly sets aside his book in order to ring me up, I've got just under a pound. I hand him a ten dollar bill, then toss the change in a jar marked as going to the county animal shelter.

Once I've paid, we sit on a bench outside the shop and I fish out the neapolitan taffies to try. I hand one to Jonah, who accepts while simultaneously telling me I don't have to share.

"So, that's one tourist attraction down. What next?" I say through my mouthful of taffy. The sugar hits my stomach hard, and I realize how little I've eaten in two days. Other than coffee, beer, and wine, the last thing I ate was a couple slices of bacon. Before that was the peanut butter toast from two nights ago. My stomach acid gurgles and churns around itself, and my vision goes dark and hot for a second.

"We could do the preserve or the beach. The place to get lobster is right on the water, we could go there next."

"I'm not really hu—" I almost lie before I realize I don't need to anymore. Jonah won't lecture me about how I should've eaten more at the diner if I were hungry. He suggested going to get food, and he won't make me feel like my bodily needs are an inconvenience. "You know what, I actually could go for some lunch."

"All right, we'll do the beach and lighthouse next then." He turns toward the car, then spins on his heels, suddenly concerned. "You have seen the ocean before, right?"

Technically, yes. I saw it on my way in, but I don't know if that counts so I shake my head. Based on his expression, I think I can safely assume he's going to keep me occupied for the rest of the afternoon. Surprisingly, the assumption comes as a relief. It'll be nice to get out of my own head for a while.

THIRTEEN

WHAT LITTLE WARMTH THE DAY HAD DISAPPEARS WHEN the sun dips behind a thick covering of gray clouds. I pull my quilted coat tighter around my body as we duck into the small restaurant Jonah brings me to. The building is made of wood that looks to have drifted ashore from a shipwreck. Nets and brightly colored buoys hang on the entire side facing the gravel parking lot. A pathway of crushed mussel and clam shells leads up to the door, painted a tired red. Fenced off with thick, coarse rope are two gardens with half dead scrubby plants and a few intentionally placed wooden lobster traps.

Evidently, this part of Maine goes very hard when it comes to their aesthetic. What a place.

There are six tables inside the dining room, which is decorated in the same nautical theme as the outside with the addition of photos of boats and traps and men holding lobsters and other sea creatures. Beside the counter, there are a few tanks full of water with brownish colored crustaceans crawling over one another. Each tank has been marked with the weight range of the lobsters inside.

The menu has a few options, and I decide to go with the lobster roll. I don't know how I'll feel about a meal that looks back at me, especially one that also requires significant effort to get to the edible parts.

Jonah orders the same, which I take as a sign I've made a good choice. We take our plastic numbers and set them on the table we choose in front of a large rectangular window overlooking the ocean. It still looks angry. Deep aqua water and frothy waves churn mere yards from the building we sit inside.

I fiddle with my plastic number in the time that passes between conversations. Silence doesn't bother me usually, but the ends of my nerves feel all frayed and I need to expel the energy. Beneath the table, my leg bounces like the motion powers the entire town.

"Is the ocean always so dark here?" I ask.

Jonah nods. "Most of the time. It's totally different from the tropics with their clear water and white sand. And it's cold. All the time."

"Interesting. It's pretty." I watch as a wave crashes against a small white boat. Only a few others bob along with it.

I set my phone face up on the table beside the number I discard, and look out the window with my chin propped on clasped hands. The only thing I can expect to come in on the device is a text from Elise, but I haven't heard from her since last night when we messaged briefly about the horse.

"It is. Definitely not the kind of beach to lounge on in the summer, though people still try. Usually they end up flocking to the dozens of little lakes and ponds outside the town boundaries in the unorganized territories. Those get warmer, and people can have a whole pond to themselves if they have the right amount of money."

"That's why people come here, isn't it? To be off the grid and connected with nature. Well, aside from the ones who come trying to figure out the murder thing."

"Yep. Off the grid, but close enough to town that they can get cell reception and basic necessities if they need."

For the first time, I understand the appeal of this place. It hadn't occurred to me that anyone would want to come here, or choose to stay, but now I get it. Being on the last civilized edge of the grid sounds amazing.

My phone starts buzzing beside me, but I ignore it. A spam caller, probably.

"Do you need to answer that?" Jonah asks, glancing down at the screen which is lit up by an incoming call from the thumbs down emoji.

"Absolutely not." I shake my head as the screen powers down. Looks like Brent gave up after a couple rings, and I don't mind not having a voicemail to delete later.

Fuck Brent.

I refuse to answer any of his calls, and decide instead to finally block his number. It's a better choice than letting him keep bothering me. Whatever he think he has to say, he should've said it before I left. Before he asked me to leave.

"Sorry about that," I say. Half the time, I don't even know what I'm apologizing for. It just comes out.

"Don't worry about it."

A middle aged woman comes by with two red plastic baskets lined with red and white checkered paper. The grilled and buttered hot dog roll overflows with lobster mixed with mayonnaise and a little salt and pepper. A pickle sits on a leaf of lettuce, and waffle fries fill the remaining space.

She leaves a bottle of ketchup and then returns to the kitchen without a word.

The call from Brent left me without an appetite, but the food looks good and my stomach aches. I lift the roll and some of the lobster tumbles out into the basket. After a few gentle squeezes to make it more compact, I take the first bite.

"Well?" Jonah points a waffle fry at me.

"Pretty good." It would feel like less of a lie if I had any interest whatsoever in food. Feeding myself feels like a chore. I don't remember a time when it hasn't. "Not something I'd eat every day."

He tells me some story about how lobster used to be considered garbage and was fed to the poor for a while. I don't really listen as he shares the history of how it became popular among tourists and richer people. I keep eating and let my thoughts drift back to the horse and to Brent and to how weird these last couple days have been.

Goddamn I am tired.

I need to rest. Maybe tomorrow I'll have a chance to sit and watch something silly and chill out, though I know the attempt will only last an hour or two at most.

It would be easy enough to feed the horse in the morning and then go back to bed. Find a book on Roger and Evie's shelves and settle in with it. Shut my phone off to all unwanted calls and messages. Ignore my toxic need to clean the house, which still looks as if no one actually lives in it.

"Are you okay?" Jonah interrupts my thoughts.

I look up at him and realize I've eaten all my food and have been staring at the bottom of the basket for who knows how long.

"Sure. Yeah." I decide at that moment I absolutely must fix my ponytail, which has come loose over the course of the day. "Tired, you know? Can't stop thinking about what I've read in Evie's journal."

He pops a chunk of loose lobster meat from his own basket into his mouth. "I bet."

"I don't know how to relax so this should be interesting, I think." I frown. "This and the bacon are the first things I've eaten since Wednesday."

"That doesn't sound great." He chooses each word carefully, like he doesn't want to come across judgmental.

"Nah, definitely not ideal, but here we are."

The hint of humor laces my voice as I seal my wounds back up, already having been more vulnerable than I'd like. Talk of my irreversibly fucked up eating habits and atrocious circadian rhythm might scare off normal people, and I can't afford to scare off the one person who seems to not mind me. I've already, in just a day, grown comfortable with this feeling of not being as alone as my empty, unlived in house suggests.

"You'll get into a routine here. I imagine moving so suddenly didn't help," he says.

"Yeah."

Everything has been so sudden. The divorce. Moving across the country. This whole thing with the horse. I could go for a slow burn with literally anything right about now. An easy start that lets me settle in before anything else chaotic happens. Even better, something without chaos.

I fix my ponytail again, smoothing the hair down in places I imagine it sticking up.

Jonah and I head outside after leaving our emptied baskets in a bin beside the trash, and I let him steer the topic of conversation away from my disaster of a life and back towards the tour he's promised me. His commentary about the black and white lighthouse set on the opposite end of the beach eases my mind again, and I settle into something closer to calm than anything I've felt in a long time. Though, through the calm screams the urge to take more control of my life instead of waiting for something to happen.

I chose to get as far from Madison as I could, but I didn't choose Bowen's Leg on my own. Elise found me a place to live that I couldn't pass up, but had I chose on my own I might have ended up somewhere warm like California or a Carolina. The closest thing to a choice I've made on my own is asking Jonah to hang out today, and I like how it feels.

"What if you helped me solve the mystery? In secret, of course," I blurt.

"What?"

"Hear me out. You hate how people portray this town when they come to investigate." I put the word 'investigate' in air quotes with my fingers. "What if we solved it together? It would give the town the chance to start over too. You can build the community you want without that horrible legend hanging over you."

Jonah considers my suggestion for a moment, and he definitely doesn't look like he plans on agreeing to my offer. It would be nice to have a partner in all this, someone who knows the town and all the players in Evie's journal, but if he declines, I'll be fine. I won't bring it up again.

"Fine. On one condition." He holds up a finger. "If anything else happens while you're in that house, you tell the police."

"Okay, fair enough."

FOURTEEN

J‍ONAH DROPS ME OFF AT HOME AS THE DAY SINKS INTO dusk. Fog hovers over the ground outside as the temperature in the air drops, and it leaves the barn looking more haunted than usual when I go out to feed. The horse lingers by the stall door after I let her back inside and retrieve her water bucket, looking out into the woods with her ears pricked forward and body rigid.

As I step back out of the house with the refilled bucket in one hand, I fit my keys between my fingers and close my fist, a defense mechanism long accepted for the crossing of parking lots and garages and walking home alone when Brent went to another bar and I decided to call it a night. Maybe not for fighting off a moose or a fucking bear or whatever, but it's the best I've got unless I want to carry the five iron wherever I go.

One of the horse's ears flicks to me as I approach, then back into the darkening woods.

I walk slowly so I won't spill any water down my jeans and so I wont spook the horse further. She stands taller than usual, tense, neck straight up and muscles twitching. She grunts when I slide open the door, then kicks at the dirt with her back hooves.

"What's out there, girl?" I ask.

My preference would be not knowing, but that isn't an option.

I kind of thought, now that I knew what I heard had been a horse, the weirdness would stop and I'd be left alone to figure out what to do next. So much for that.

When the horse doesn't move, not even another twitch of the ear at the sound of my voice, I set the water bucket on the ground and take my phone out and turn the light on. It shines between the trees and I move closer and closer to them, but I find nothing except a vicious chill that sinks deep into my bones. The hair on the back of my neck stands up, as alert as the horse, and my gut tells me to stop walking.

I move the beam of light from side to side, hoping to catch a shadow or another ghostly figure—at least part of one—to prove there really is something here. The horse's behavior would be enough normally, but I don't know her well enough yet and this has gone on for days now.

"Whatever you're doing, it isn't funny," I yell into the darkness. "Get a fucking hobby or something."

A blur at the edge of the light makes me turn on my heels too fast. A grayish figure, tall and vaguely shaped like a person—slender and lanky—moves past me with a chill and I lose my balance, but catch myself with an extended arm on a nearby tree. Beneath my hand, the tree's coarse bark bites the soft skin of my palm and I wince. Fuck.

I look frantically for the thing that rushed past me, but I find only trees, bushes, stones. Branches bent at odd angles look like arms reaching up from the ground, desperately hoping to grasp something sturdy and drag the rest of their figure out of the deep soil.

No.

There isn't anything out here.

It was definitely a person.

No, I'm imagining this.

The horse probably caught scent of a squirrel or perhaps the lights form Jonah's car did something strange to the shadows in the fog.

If I stay out here, wandering around in the thickening darkness looking for something that isn't real, I'll hurt myself.

I turn, pulling my hand off the tree that caught me and head back into the yard. The horse runs full force along the perimeter of the fence. I thought I locked her inside for the night. Didn't I? Now I can't remember the sensation of the metal latch moving into the locked position beneath my hands. Doubt creeps in.

The horse shrieks and kicks every now and then. I have to calm her down before she breaks out of the fence or breaks a leg. I can't deal with any of that right now. She's my responsibility for now, regardless of where she came from and how she got here.

My ankle rolls as I hurry to find the switches for the flood lights on the outside of the barn, and I curse. This place is trying to kill me, it seems. Not in any particularly gruesome way, but it's trying none the less. Blunt force trauma or something equally boring and not all that dramatic. Sounds like a reasonable way for me to go out.

The flood lights cast the pasture in gold and turn the fog into shimmering clouds. The horse slows, but not enough. She paces the edge of the fence closest to the trees and keeps her focus fixed on the places the light doesn't reach.

I head out into the pasture and approach the horse slowly, speaking in a calm voice to her so I won't spook her even more and end up trampled. It takes a few minutes for her to chill out and approach me, nosing at my injured palm in hopes of finding a treat. I lead her to her stall and lock the door, then bring her water and food for the night.

Whatever she sensed that got her all riled up fades from her mind as soon as she sees her food. Meanwhile, my chest aches from stress about all the worst case scenarios of the horse injuring herself while running or of a masked murderer emerging from the woods. I saw something. At least, I felt its presence.

I reach into my jacket pocket for my keys to bring them inside with me when I realize they're gone. "Shit." Frantic, I pat my jeans as if the pockets can fit anything bigger than a lip balm in them.

Did I set them down with the water bucket? I return to the barn's entrance and look on the ground, but find no trace of them. All the places I could have put them in the barn fail me. They're not atop the tool box or on the hood of the covered car.

I must have dropped them in the woods, and there is no way I'm going back out there tonight.

Ugh. When do I get the break I came here for?

I sulk across the yard and back into the house, which miraculously hasn't locked itself while I was out chasing shadows. It wouldn't surprise me. At this point, nothing would surprise me.

With a can of seltzer in hand, I sink into the couch and open Evie's journal even though I'm not in the best head-space for what she has to tell me. My whole body feels full of bees. Even Beef doesn't want to hang out with me in my current state.

Evie writes about visiting Benjamin several more times,

and seems to revel in how he goes from a complete man to a decayed husk of one. The progression of Benjamin's downfall leaves me feeling a bit sick. It feels wrong to read this journal and not tell someone, even though I know it wouldn't do any good. Benjamin is gone and so is Evie.

He was dead today.

The next words I read stand out, stark black ink against the yellowed white paper, and confirm what I already know: nothing I do can change whatever she's already done.

It didn't take as long as I expected for his physical form to lose strength and become dead weight. I found it lying against the tall, granite boulder I left him bound to with thick ropes I found in the barn. His skin had long taken on a grayish shade alongside the bruises, but his discarded body looked more like the nearby stone after the departure of his soul. He felt the needle go in as I injected the poison into his blood, where it would travel to broken bones and cause infection.

He felt his organs fail, his body begin to rot, and the worms begin to devour him while he could do no more than try endlessly to break free. He felt his life bleed into the soil below him, nourishing the things beneath.

His ghost hovered at the very edge of his reach, a blur of translucent gray. I spoke to him, but he couldn't respond. He could only linger, helpless. I told him he'd remain there forever, like a stain on the forest, held captive by his own poisoned bones.

Benjamin is dead, but not gone.

I reread Evie's description of Benjamin's form after the

death of his body. "A blur of translucent gray" sticks with me.

Could he still be here?

If he is, how did he reach me all the way out here when Evie said he only had a small territory in the woods to roam?

All of this is ridiculous. None of the information matches up, unless I accept that what I've been experiencing and what Evie writes about are two separate things.

I get up to grab another drink from the fridge and do a double take as I pass the iron hook where I normally hang my keys. I had them in my hands when I went outside. They served as half-assed Wolverine claws to protect me from creeps in the woods, and I dropped them while searching for said creep. I know I had them, and I know I lost them.

But they hang on the second hook from the door, the one I naturally hang my keys on out of habit because that was my hook back in Madison. Not gone. Not lost. The keys are where they belong, and now I don't know if any of what I remember about tonight was ever real.

FIFTEEN

IT DOESN'T TAKE LONG FOR THE MORNINGS TO FEEL LIKE A time loop. I wake every day to Beef curled up against my stomach, and he complains when I finally drag myself out of bed to shower. Then I feed and water the horse while the coffee brews. I drink two, sometimes three, cups of coffee while pacing tracks in the floor from the coffee pot to the couch and back until Beef gets agitated with my constant movement and claws at the leg of my jeans as I pass. The small bones in my right hand grow sore from holding Evie's journal while I walk.

I give Jonah the rundown on key events in Evie's journal via text. So far, I know she did something to Benjamin to curse him to the same spot in the forest forever, his body decayed, and his soul remained in the woods. She gave us a few waypoints leading to his altar, as she calls it, and I make note of them. The abandoned truck, the U shaped tree.

He supplements my information with commonly known details from the legend, as well as sections of a knockoff wikipedia page—creatively named Lorepedia—for the story.

As much as I know he doesn't like what I've asked him to do, he doesn't complain. Another couple days and I might even say he's becoming interested in the case.

Asshat:
[pasted from Lorepedia] Eveline Ouellette, born Eveline Drinkwater, was born in 1972. She married Roger Ouellette in 1991.

[pasted from Lorepedia] Shortly after her marriage to Ouellette, Eveline was a suspect in the disappearance of Benjamin Vincent—husband of Eveline's longtime friend, Betty Campbell. Betty vanished and was declared dead in late 1992 when her car was found in a nearby lake. Her body has not been recovered. Though Benjamin had been questioned, he was not suspected in her disappearance or her death.

[pasted from Lorepedia] After giving birth to two children with Ouellette, Eveline herself disappeared and has not been seen or heard from since 1994.

Marisa:
Yikes.

The timelines on Lorepedia are about the only useful things on there. When I follow the links that accompany what Jonah texts me while he's passing time at work, I find speculation that varies in its absurdity. Some people actually believe Evie and Benjamin were taken by aliens, turned into werewolves, *were* werewolves to begin with and had to flee after killing Betty, and all this other stuff I can't wrap my head around.

Even after everything that's happened, I still have limits, I guess.

I run out of grain a few days after Jonah brought the initial bag. Despite texting him regularly about the Evie stuff, I've been avoiding going to see him in person. The thought of going to the farm and garden store makes me feel weird. I've convinced myself he'll think I came out just for him, and that whole concept cranks up my awkwardness even if it is totally irrational. What if he thinks I'm into him? What if I'm coming on too strong?

With the empty bag in the barn and the walls of the house closing in on me, I have to go out. The change of scenery will be good for me, and the drive will give me a new place to think.

How did Evie curse Benjamin?

I did Google it, but the internet did not contain anything particularly useful. If it were that easy to find the exact steps to curse a man to a miserable eternity stuck in the woods, I suppose more people would have done it. Right?

"Well, Beef." I hike my pants up from where they hang too low on my hips. "I guess I'm out of here. You're in charge. Keep the ghosts away, all right?"

The cat neither accepts nor acknowledges his assignment. Typical.

I triple check the door behind me to be sure it's securely locked, then speed walk to the car. I'm on edge, even now in the daylight. I hate this feeling, but I can't remember the last time I felt truly safe. Before the fear of some mysterious being hanging out in the woods, there was always the looming threat of Brent coming home before I'd gotten around to finishing the housework. Or worse, when I'd given myself a break for a depression nap.

Those naps were the only time I ever slept, despite the nagging of the dinner prep I hadn't started or the load of laundry sitting in the dryer with wrinkles settling deep into the fabric.

He never hit me, but somehow the weight of the guilt he made me feel stung worse than any slap across the face.

I won't let myself think about Brent too. There are so many other things, like how my car shudders a little too long and I wonder if this might be the last time it starts.

I back out of the driveway and an image of me riding the horse into town with saddlebags full of groceries and other standard bullshit, a cup of coffee in my hand floats through my mind. A bitter laugh escapes my lungs. Ridiculous.

I might be losing my goddamn mind.

"Stay with me, car." I pat the steering wheel.

The farm and garden store has more cars than usual, mostly trucks, and relief comes over me. Jonah will be busy. I won't have to risk spending too much time talking, since I've also gotten it in my head that he's mad at me for making him help me solve Evie's mystery and that he regrets befriending me because I'm awful or something.

I hate the feeling of knowing I'll disappoint someone. It's like standing on a ledge and looking down knowing there's no way back up once you fall.

Once inside the store, I go straight to the aisle dedicated to horses and pick up a bag of grain and a plastic container of apple and oat treats. At the checkout, the cashier—a white, ruddy-cheeked lady maybe in her early forties— rings me up and sends me on my way without much in the way of pleasantries.

I haven't seen Jonah anywhere yet, though I think I remember him saying he'd be here. Come to think of it, I hadn't noticed his car in the lot either. Could he have told me he was working so I wouldn't bug him? Because he doesn't like me?

The cashier doesn't offer to help me with my purchases, so I haul the bag over one shoulder and take the container of treats in my free hand along with my keys.

"You were just going to leave without saying hi?" Jonah's voice comes from somewhere behind me.

He, again, holds too many objects in one hand—this time two quarts of paint—and a pang of nervousness shoots through my heart at the thought of them falling and spilling. He has two hands. Why is he not using them?

"Um, you make it sound way more intentional than it is." My eyes linger on the paint.

He sets the cans on the counter where I'd just been standing, then hurries to help me with the grain bag.

I should ask if he knows when his friends will come to take the horse.

I do no such thing.

"You good today?" he asks after tossing the bag in the trunk of the SUV.

"Sure. Yeah. Frazzled, maybe."

He leans against my car and sticks his hands in the pockets of his jeans. "Has anything happened?"

I don't tell him about my keys or about the apparition, and I don't tell him I didn't call the police. Neither event seemed to warrant calling the cops to check out the property.

"Nah, I've been really into the first bit of Evie's journal though. Kinda dark stuff."

He nods. "Yeah, it's not great."

"I thought I was in a shitty headspace with the divorce and all that but she's definitely worse. Maybe that means I'm coping better than I thought."

"Of course you are."

Jonah smiles in that crooked way that makes the skin at the corners of his eyes crinkle a little. It makes me want to apologize for being weird today and accidentally avoiding him. It's a warm and welcoming expression, one that says *keep telling me about your day.* I almost want to stay, but another customer approaches and requires his attention so I have to go. I really should go.

"Oh, hey I almost forgot." he turns and calls back to me. "My friends, Hellie and Jack, can come by tomorrow with the trailer. Does that work for you?"

I give what is apparently now my signature move: a thumbs up, and he returns the gesture. Then, he disappears into the store with his customer, who has already started talking to him before our conversation really ends.

CHAPTER

SIXTEEN

Since the horse will be leaving tomorrow, I decide to take the afternoon off from studying Evie's journal and whatever the internet has for speculation about what happened. For a while, I stand by the fence with the leftover coffee from this morning and watch while the horse wanders the pasture in search of grass or plants to nibble on, though nothing has started growing this early in the spring.

My leg bounces, restless, and I fiddle with the seam on the side of my jeans. My body buzzes with anxiety, and I wonder if I should take up running to burn off the pent up energy within me.

When I finish my coffee, I set the mug on the ground beside the fencepost and head into the barn for my lead and a halter Jonah's friends had him drop off. I decide I'll see what the horse already knows. If she recognizes the feel of the halter on her head and my instruction to walk at the end of my line, it means someone has done some training with her. She might even be rideable, not that I have any intention on trying that any time soon. Not without supervision. At least working her will keep me out of my head and let the information I have settle.

When I approach, she lets out a huff I can't interpret. I resist the urge to back away when she shakes her head and digs a front hoof into the ground like a bull about to charge.

"Knock it off," I say, firm. Animals sense fear and take advantage of it, so I banish any trace of it from my voice.

She tries to bite me, catches the fabric of my sweater between her teeth, and I kick her gently in the shin with the toe of my boot. The surprise gives her a jolt, and she retreats. Her eyes hold betrayal in them, as if she can't believe I'd defend myself.

I'm the boss. I'm in charge here.

The horse stills, but a glimmer of something fiery replaces the betrayal in her dark eyes. She remains patient while I strap the halter in place, and even stands politely when I attach the lead to her.

"Walk," I order.

The horse looks at me like she can't understand what I want from her.

"You know how to walk," I say. "You did it the other day."

Okay, fine. So she didn't do the best job walking when I brought her out to pasture when Jonah and I first examined her, but she knew what I wanted.

"Let's go. Walk."

She stands firmly in place. I take a step toward her and tug her halter in the direction I want her go.

Still nothing.

Again, I pull her forward. "Walk." Both my tone and the

way I gesture for her to move must be stronger now, because she responds with a single step forward.

Finally, she moves along with me, though not very well. Her attention strays with every new and interesting thing she finds in the brown grass. I fish through my jeans pocket for one of the lumpy oat treats and click my tongue to get her attention.

Again, I give the command to walk, and when she does, I offer her the treat with a flat palm like my very first instructor taught me. Even now, twenty years later, I hear her voice. *Horses don't always know the difference between fingers and carrots!* She tried saying it with cheer in her voice, but that didn't change how absolutely terrifying the thought of having my fingers chomped off was to little me.

She accepts the treat, then noses at my hand in search of more goodies.

I tell her no and take a few steps away before extracting another treat from my pocket. The horse learns — or remembers — quickly when there's food involved. After all the cookies in my pockets, she's figured out how to walk beside me without being pulled. She responds to 'walk' and 'stop' like she's been doing it her whole life, and even discovers a trace of the scent of her treats coming off my jeans. She nibbles at my pockets where they used to be.

"You're a terrible creature. You know that, right?"

I push her away from me and begin walking toward the barn for dinner. Since I already have her geared up, it makes sense to bring her in instead of letting her do it on her own terms. That never ends well. Half the time, I end up waiting well into the night for her to decide she's done roaming outside.

The horse grumbles when I close the door behind us, but doesn't kick like I expect her to. Taking off the halter goes easier than getting it on, as does refilling her feed bucket and situating a bucket of warm water from the house in a place where she might not knock it over. It surprises me. The last couple nights, she's been a total terrorist. All around, not a great horse. Very shrieky and kicky and awful.

"Thanks for not being too much of an asshole today," I say as I slide her stall door shut and lock it.

In response, I hear her dig around in her grain bucket and spill the contents on the ground beside it. Can't win them all, I guess.

A chill in the air bites at my forearms, bare from rolling my sleeves up to my elbows. Instead of rolling them down, I skip folding the chair I'd left on the lawn and carry it assembled back to the house. It saves all of two seconds, and probably slows me down more anyway. Logic doesn't matter. I'm tired and ready to settle in for the night with a bowl of popcorn. Not the instant, microwave stuff, but the kind you make in a pan with butter and salt and everything seasoning, if you're feeling particularly fancy.

The win with the horse leaves me feeling like I deserve to toss in a bunch of seasoning while the kernels pop. I even wash the few dishes in the sink, which are mostly peanut butter smeared knives from when I remembered to feed myself. It feels, for a second, like I've stepped out of an unlit room to greet the sun for the first time in a year.

Then my phone rings.

Brent. Again.

I thought I blocked him the day he called me in the lobster restaurant. I know I did.

I tap the screen with a thumb and answer it, which is an action not even my good mood could have prepared me to take. If someone said I'd answer his call, I'd've laughed in their face and claimed I wouldn't ever be so stupid.

Except I did it.

"Marisa? You there?" he says when I don't actually say anything.

Way to ruin your own damn day, Marisa. You could've let it go to voicemail again. You could have re-blocked his number.

"Yeah."

How do I talk to this person who shattered me like glass and abandoned me to clean up their mess? I want to spit venom. To hurt him like he hurt me. I want to make him feel smaller than he ever made me feel.

"Where are you?" he asks.

"Does it matter?" I say. "What do you want?"

I remove the pan with the popcorn from the heat and dump the fluffy contents into the biggest bowl I can find.

"I'm trying to sell the house."

"Cool. Good for you. I don't care." I bite the inside of my cheek to keep my tone in check. "What do you need from me then? I'm not on any of the paperwork, remember?"

It would be amazing to be able to strangle a man through the phone. Not that I have any interest in really committing a crime against him. I've had enough consequences from marrying him. I don't need to be thrown in jail now.

"I know. Listen though." He uses a voice I remember so well. It's his I'm gonna convince you to do something you don't want to do, and I'm gonna do it through guilt voice. It worked so fucking well. He used that voice for everything, from picking up the dry cleaning that was on his way home from work to having subpar sex to baking his buddy's favorite dessert for some gathering I would then be forced to attend to keep up appearances.

I cram a fistful of popcorn into my mouth, playing at

being disinterested in hopes of it coming through the phone. I don't care. I don't care. I don't care.

"The water heater's busted. Needs to be fixed before I can sell. I was hoping you could help cover the cost. You did take longer showers and used extra hot water for dishes and stuff, it's only fair. Like, I wasn't alone in breaking it."

What.

The fuck.

"Are you —" the unpopped kernel in my throat interrupts me for a moment. "Are you fucking serious right now?"

I think I understand Evie's rage after all. The burning emotion that drove her to curse Benjamin. If he weren't hundreds of miles away, would I do the same thing to Brent? Is that why I'm so drawn to the journal? Because I too have the makings of a man killer within me?

Maybe I'm a terrible person for thinking that, but it makes me feel a little better knowing that a cursed Brent trapped out in the middle of the woods wouldn't be able to call me and ask for money.

"It's a lot of money to fix, Rissa. I need to sell this house."

I cringe at the nickname he used to use for me.

"Don't call me that. You can call me Marisa or you can simply not call me at all." I wish I could laugh at myself for being hilarious and petty. Fuck, I am talented. Brilliant.

Yet, my hands tremble like an earthquake rages in my bones.

"Please. I wouldn't ask if it wasn't important."

"Let me get settled out here on my own, then we'll talk."

I end the call, and set the phone beside my popcorn. What this meal needs now is wine. Wine to ease my nerves. Wine to blur over the fact that I gave him a way in and let him think I'm going to help. I left the door wide open.

SEVENTEEN

THE AMOUNT OF WINE I DRINK SHOULD KNOCK ME OUT, but instead I lie awake in my bed, sweaty and tangled in the sheets. I obsess over the fact that I still, after everything, let Brent guilt me into believing I need to help him. I know how much a water heater can cost to repair, because I remember seeing the bill Dad forgot to file away when ours broke back when I was in high school. If it's anything like that, Brent could be expecting thousands of dollars from me.

I can't give him that. I won't.

I shouldn't have let him think I'd consider it.

How do I even know he's telling the truth. I don't. Static fills my head as I try and come up with reasons why he'd lie, though I don't need one. He'd lie because he likes to see what he can get away with. Because I'm a fucking sucker and I've never said no to him before. Why start now?

Beef sits on the couch and glares at me when I scuffle past him to get a glass of water. I must have bothered him with my tossing and turning if he's out here holding a grudge.

"Sorry dude," I grumble. The cat turns his head away from me, ignoring the apology. Petty little shit.

Outside, the sky glows like fire in shades of yellow and orange and red. The sun peeks just over the treeline, casting everything in brilliant morning light. My eyes ache from not sleeping, or maybe from the wine, but I take in the beauty anyway.

Water from the glass spills down my face as I drink the entire thing too fast. It makes my insides feel almost alive again instead of shriveled and dried up. There's no point in trying to go back to sleep now with the contents of my stomach sloshing like a storm. May as well get up and do something with the horse, since that made me feel kind of good yesterday.

I make a pot of coffee despite knowing the only solution to my current miserable state of existence is water, ibuprofen, and probably sleep. Though I could save the water water and simply go outside and be a human salt lick with the sweat dried up on my arms, I shower while the coffee brews and rub the crust from my eyes and the corners of my mouth. I'm such a catch.

With dripping hair and still wrapped up in my towel, I rummage through the medicine cabinet for some kind of headache remedy. Now is one of those times I wish I'd gotten the preparedness gene from my father. If he were here, he'd have a hideous fanny pack with everything one could possibly need tucked neatly inside. He'd hand me an individual pack of Advil and, when I couldn't open it with my stubby nails, he'd whip out the little scissors on his multi-tool to help.

My chest aches that I can't turn to him for help now. I need him, and he's gone. I wasted the last years I had with him in Madison while he was losing strength in South Dakota.

No. I can't think like that right now.

I can't.

I slam the cabinet when I find nothing useful and then move on to the drawers beneath the sink.

Well, at least there's plenty of toilet paper in this house.

Giving up on my search for painkillers, I get dressed and go into the kitchen for my coffee. If it weren't so hot still, I'd drink it straight from the carafe. All of it.

Instead, I dump ice in a mug and pour the hot liquid over it. Three cups of watered down, over-sugared black coffee does little beyond making me more dehydrated and alert. The bitter liquid of the fourth cup makes me sick, and I dump it down the drain. The smell lingers, slightly burnt and sharp in my now-awake nostrils.

I retch.

The empty wine bottle sits in the sink filled with soapy water, but I swear I can smell the scent of $8 fermented grapes with notes of the wood it sat in for years.

Bile comes up fast and I only barely make it back to the sink. My stomach seizes and twitches like it wants to go again as I run water to rinse away the mess. I grab a paper towel and blow my nose, bile burning its way up my nasal passage on the way out. I haven't felt this sick since college, when I was naive enough to get bombed on watermelon vodka without worrying what Brent's business major friends would do if I passed out. Oh, those were the days.

Vaguely, I remember opening the bottle of wine last night. It was one of three cheap bottles I bought at the grocery store, and, because of Brent, it's already gone.

When I look for the bowl of popcorn, I find I barely ate

any of it. The bowl sits on the coffee table where I left it, only a few handfuls eaten. Popped kernels are scattered around the table's surface and on the floor. Among the popcorn, I find dirt stomped into the wood floor, along with the curled up body of a dead house centipede. Gross. Did I go outside last night?

I can't bend to clean the mess without my stomach lurching.

Ugh. I should know better.

When my stomach settles from leaning down to inspect the mess I left on the floor, I pour another glass of room temperature water and drag myself to the couch. The coffee only made me feel worse, so I nudge Beef until he gives me enough room to lay on my side. Eventually he curls up into me. His anger at Mother for disturbing his sleep cannot overshadow his need to care for Mother when she is ill. He purrs like a rocket against my lungs, and I stroke the soft fur between his ears until the room stops spinning.

I stay there for a while, long enough to almost dip into unconsciousness, but not quite. The water remains untouched on the table, but the jittery feeling of too much coffee eventually settles down. When I don't feel like I've been shaken, I consider getting up.

Jonah and his friends are coming today, and right now I can barely stand. I have to get my shit together.

Instead I pick up Evie's journal and open it to where I last left off, but I can't focus. As I inch closer to sober, I try and rationalize the fact that I told Brent I'd give him money. Self-preservation skills? I don't know them. He could ask me to carry his child for nine months and my dumb ass would consider it. Thankfully, that shit isn't in the cards anymore.

The more I think about the last almost decade of my life, the more I want to vomit. I lost my father to an incurable disease. I lost my husband to a string of girls before one who seems actually pretty cool. She's like nineteen or something the legal side of creepy. Influencer gorgeous. I hope someone saves her like I wish someone had saved me, because she doesn't deserve him in the way raccoons don't deserve to be hit by cars. I hope she figures that out.

I should call Brent and tell him to take his water heater and shove it up his ass.

My stomach gives me three seconds to get off the couch and reach the toilet, interrupting my pity party, and I consider promising myself I'll never drink again. Instead, I doze off against the side of tub, one arm draped over the toilet, Beef pressed up against my feet.

CHAPTER

EIGHTEEN

SINCE IT'S UNREASONABLY EARLY TO EXPECT JONAH AND his friends to arrive, even after my hour long nap on the bathroom floor, I decide to try reading the journal again. I force myself to eat two pieces of plain toast with the lukewarm water I've poured myself, then settle in on the couch. My head aches enough that I text Jonah and beg him to pick up ibuprofen on his way over. At least I can read to pass the time.

> *I haven't written or gone to see Benjamin in a few days. I've been in bed, sick with a terrible head cold. Roger said I shouldn't be outside for so long, not that he knows anything about why I go out into the woods. He can't know. Nonetheless, he suspects my illness has something to do with my frequent long walks through the forest.*
>
> *The doctor said it's just a cold. I only need a little while to rest and recover.*

I take my mother's remedy of a few drops of garlic extract twice per day so I can go check on the altar soon.

Sometimes, I forget the woman telling me her story was telling it from the nineties. She isn't some centuries old legend passed down from generation to generation. She died only years before I was born, assuming she did actually die. She was in my dad's generation. It blows my mind when I remember that detail.

She dates the entries, and her entry about the cold comes almost two weeks after she found Benjamin's body separated from his soul.

The next entry comes after a few days, though it's short and indicates she's still sick and Roger has begun worrying. She says he's threatened to take her to a doctor outside of town, since the ones in town are already biased against her.

The medicine the city doctor gave me makes me feel invincible. I bet I can walk to Benjamin in half the time it normally takes.

Another week passes before she sees Benjamin again. Her handwriting has changed significantly, like her dominant hand has grown tired from holding her pen and she decided to try writing with the other.

Something went wrong.
I saw him out there, not a ghost anymore but a real man. His body still laid on the ground with insects crawling out of what used to be his eye sockets, but he stood beside it.
Something went wrong.
He smiled at me when he noticed me among the trees, like he had heard a very satisfying joke moments before I arrived.

He said nothing to me when I arrived, but I felt his spirit tugging on mine.

He shouldn't be able to take my strength, but I felt his roots clashing with my own as if he intended to regain what I took from him. He won't succeed.

I don't like the sound of this, and I read the entry again to be sure I read it correctly. I don't know what it means or how Benjamin's soul could possibly drain Evie of her life force.

My phone buzzes with a text from Jonah.

Asshat:
Hellie and Jack will be there in an hour. I'm on my way with ibuprofen.

With Jonah incoming, I close the journal, but not before I notice a smear of brownish-red beside a chunk of handwriting in the next entry.

To show him I was not playing any games, I removed two fingers from his corpse. He can't be set free from here unless his entire body is cleansed. The fingers will serve as reassurance that his soul will never be free.

Gross.

I glance back at the smear on the page.

Oh my god, it looks like dried blood. What if it is?

With that, I shut the journal with a clap of the covers. The thought of removing a piece of a dead body and carrying it home makes me want to vomit again, and I've done enough of that this morning in my extremely hungover state. Did she put the fingers in her pocket or keep them held in her hand? Where did she put them when she got back? Oh god, are there two loose fingers somewhere in the house?

Jonah arrives a few minutes after I turn my attention to cat memes on my phone, and I explain to him why I desperately needed the palate cleanser of illiterate felines. I don't, however, explain to him why I need the ibuprofen even though I'm half convinced the house smells like puke.

"Why has no one read this journal?" I ask Jonah as he flips through it with a troubled expression on his face. "Wouldn't it have been evidence in an investigation or something?"

He shakes his head, causing a wavy tendril of hair to fall into his eye.

"There was no investigation. You may have noticed we don't exactly have a ton of police resources around here. According to official records, Benjamin left town after Betty died. As for Evie, the town thought she was, at best, a murderer and, at worst, a witch, but there was no proof. Sure, it was the nineties but being a witch still wasn't great. People were still recovering from the whole Satanic Panic thing around when this happened."

"Okay, but plenty of people have informally investigated this. How am I the first person to read this?" My stomach gurgles as I speak, and I hope Jonah can't hear it.

"Roger kept the journalists and bloggers and paranormal investigators away. I'm not kidding when I say the entire town hated him and Evie and their family. Things were so messed up, their two kids were sent to live with a relative out of state. They were little then."

"No wonder they want nothing to do with this place," I say.

It dawns on me then that I truly am the first person to have opened this journal in a long time. If I believed in fate, maybe I'd say I was meant to come here and put the legend to bed once and for all. I don't believe in fate, though, so the entire scenario feels completely surreal to me.

Jonah asks me questions about what I read, what I think it means, and then turns to his phone. I watch over his shoulder as he tries to search different types of curses on the internet. Curses that require a whole body to dispel, curses that cause immortality. Things I've already searched before. I don't tell him he won't find anything useful, because I'd rather let him spin his wheels if it means I won't have to talk about this anymore today.

While he reads, I keep thinking about the potential of a random guy's fingers being somewhere in my house. I imagine all the places they could be, like in a drawer in the kitchen, under the bathroom sink behind all the rolls of toilet paper, or maybe in the locked room I haven't seen. What would I do if I found them? God, I don't want to think about it. I hope they stay hidden.

No wonder Roger's kids let me live here for free. No one in their right mind would choose to live here if they knew what the town says about this place, regardless of whether they read the journal. If not for the financial value of the property, they'd probably rather it be destroyed.

But I'm a strong, independent woman and I walked myself right into the setting of a horror movie.

CHAPTER

NINETEEN

Hellie and Jack arrive an hour later, as promised by Jonah, with a trailer hitched to their burgundy GMC pickup. I'd expected people close to my age, since Jonah referred to the couple as his friends, but they're old enough to be our parents. Jack has gray hair and looks a bit like the guy from NCIS—Dad's favorite show—except a bit younger. Hellie wears her honey colored hair with a touch of white at the temples in a ponytail, and exits the truck followed by two brown and white pit bulls.

We go outside to meet them at the truck, and the dogs remain politely seated at Hellie's side.

The woman smiles wide, exposing bright white teeth, and offers a friendly wave instead of a handshake.

"You must be Marisa," she says. "Jonah has mentioned you a few times now. It's good to see him spending time with someone his own age."

"It's nice to meet you. Thank you for being willing to

take the horse. I don't ... I really don't know how to explain any of this without sounding nuts, but I guess that's to be expected around here."

"Jonah let us know the circumstances. Honestly, Jack and I are surprised it wasn't something spooky."

Jack nods, but doesn't take his eyes off the barn. "Lots of spooky stuff around here."

Spooky is an understatement, though I don't say that out loud. I don't know how much Jonah has told them about how I've decided to pass my time here.

"Oh, these are our dogs. I hope it's okay we brought them. They go everywhere with us and I loaded them into the truck without even thinking. The one with unaltered ears is Peony, and the one with her ears cropped—from prior to when my daughter adopted her, to be clear—is Lilac. Appearances aside, they are the least intimidating dogs on the planet and behave more like cats, if you ask me. They'll lounge on their bed all day if you let them."

I try not to acknowledge the fact that she insinuated the dogs have their own bed.

"They're more than welcome. Though, my cat might try and fight them."

Jack laughs from his belly. "Your cat will win."

"Seriously. The cat hates me," Jonah adds. "He glares at me the whole time I'm here."

A wave of nervousness comes over me at Jonah's comment. Do Hellie and Jack think we're *together* together, or do they know we're friends? Are they his parents? Is that why they're so delighted to see him hanging out with me? Oh no, does Jonah know we're friends, and not romantic? What if he thinks this is more? How much time do they think he spends here? Why would he call his parents by their first names?

"Beef doesn't hate you. He's asserting his dominance," I

say through the barrage of anxious thoughts in my head. "He's a good cat."

Hellie nods. "All cats are good cats."

I like her.

"What do you say we go load this horse up?" Jack says.

"Sure, let's go. You can drive the truck up the lawn if it's easier." I point to the barn. "It's a bit far and she isn't the most cooperative horse."

Hellie and Jack get back in the truck, while the dogs follow me and Jonah as we walk behind. The humming of the truck's engine serves as background noise to a question that hasn't left my head since I saw these two people exit the truck.

"Are they, um ..." Why does it feel like such a strange question? "Are they your parents?"

"May as well be, but no. My parents moved to Florida as soon as I was old enough to do my own thing. We talk on Christmas and birthdays only." He doesn't sound upset about it. He states his relationship with his parents as fact, nothing more. "Hellie and Jack had a daughter, Bri. She was my best friend growing up so I was always over their house. Even before my parents moved, they were mentally checked out. I felt more at home at Bri's anyway, and Hellie and Jack pretty much raised me."

"What happened to her? To Bri, I mean."

"She died five years ago." He looks away, gaze settling on the woods and a muscle in his jaw twitches. There's more to the story of his friend's death, but I doubt he wants to talk about it.

"Oh, I'm sorry."

The conversation fizzles, but we've reached the barn so it can't get more awkward than it already was thanks to me. Hellie asks me to help her get the horse ready for transport while Jonah and Jack prepare the trailer. Eagerly, I lead her inside to where the horse is chewing the top of the wooden half door to her stall. I show Hellie where I hung the lead and halter she lent me, and she grabs it. While she does, I kick the horse's buckets to the side so they won't get in our way. As I do, the movement startles a mouse, who darts across the stall into a hole in the wood. I don't mention it to Hellie.

The two of us don't talk much aside from asking one another for help, and the horse actually cooperates with us as we place a halter over her head and clip the lead to it.

"She's really calm," Hellie says. "Considering she was dumped here under mysterious circumstances. You've done a good job taking care of her."

I laugh, quietly so as to not startle the horse. "She's been a handful, honestly."

"Typical mare."

"Totally."

I tug on the horse's lead, and she follows me and Hellie outside to where the back of the trailer gapes open. When I get her to the ramp, she stops.

"Come on, it's okay," I say as I pet the side of her head. "They're gonna take you to a new home where there's some other horses."

She does not move.

Jack takes the lead, while Jonah distances himself from all the things occurring around him. He stands back with the dogs flanking him and scratches between their ears.

The horse rears up when Jack tugs her toward the trailer, and Hellie steps back. The two try and calm the horse down, to no avail, while I stand to the side. For some reason, my body refuses to go help. My feet anchor me to the ground and I watch Hellie and Jack attempt to get the horse to stop freaking out. She kicks with her back legs in the air, then flails her front hooves in front of her.

"Shit. I'm sorry. How can I help?" I manage to say.

"We've got her. Keep the dogs back, and make sure Jonah doesn't pass out. He's got a bit of a phobia," Jack says, still managing to throw a light jab at Jonah in that fatherly way my dad used to with me.

I do as I'm told, going to stand back where Jonah has stopped petting the dogs and crossed his arms tight across his chest.

The horse does not calm down, nor does she show interest in any of the treats Jack retrieves from his pocket. She keeps thrashing until eventually she manages to throw Jack off balance. He loses grip on the lead as he tries to steady himself, and the horse takes her opportunity to dart towards the treeline, where she stands and stares at us from the shadows.

Hellie and I rush in her direction while Jack shuts the barn door. I open the gate to the pasture while Hellie gets a firm hold on the lead and somehow convinces her to come back. We lock her in and unhook the lead, then she runs full speed in circles in her enclosure like she usually does when she loses her mind.

I watch her, not sure what to do now. Hellie's leadline feels heavy in my hands as the horse jumps and kicks the air, making horrible horse shrieks to punctuate the silence.

"We'll have to leave her for now," Hellie says, brushing her hands on the thighs of her jeans. "I can ask our vet for a sedative, then we'll try again."

"Okay." I don't have anything else to say.

"You seem to have experience with horses, but don't take any chances with her," Jack says, brushing dirt off the back of his jeans.

"Okay."

The horse keeps tearing through the pasture to the point where the grass could catch fire and I wouldn't be surprised. She doesn't slow down or show any signs of getting tired.

"I can have Jonah bring you a couple better buckets for her, in the meantime. It looks like she keeps tipping the shallow one and spilling it," Hellie says.

I nod. "Thanks."

I wring my hands, not sure what to do or say now. This went terribly. Worse than I expected, and embarrassment creeps up my neck and to my cheeks. I should have left them alone and dealt with this myself. She's been unpredictable since she arrived. I should have warned Hellie and Jack about that.

"I'm sorry I wasted your time and made you come all the way out here. I didn't know she was—" I gesture at the animal raging through the field.

I want to cry. These people probably hate me. Jack might've hurt himself falling. Jonah's traumatized.

None of them will ever talk to me again and I'm still stuck with this horse. Of all the things I don't need right now, a horse is very high on the list. Not that I have a choice in the matter anymore.

TWENTY

WITH MY HOPE OF RELIEF FROM THE RESPONSIBILITY OF caring for a horse shattered, I feed the animal and retreat back to the couch to sulk. Hellie and Jack left after I told them I'd be fine, though they promised to lend me some proper buckets for the horse. Jonah took off shortly after when I told him I needed to nap. He had questions behind his eyes, but didn't ask them. For that, I'm thankful.

Now, I lay on my side under a chunky wool blanket, ibuprofen rushing through my veins and chipping away at the ache in my head. All the lingering caffeine from the coffee I drank competes with my exhaustion, and ultimately wins the battle. My hands shake and behind my eyes feels staticky as caffeine jitters rush through me like electricity.

I should text Elise. I haven't heard from her in a while, but for some reason I don't feel like anything I have to say would make sense to her. Nothing has gotten better since I moved out here, only worse in different ways. So I've gotten away from Brent, and maybe I've made a friend, but things are still a total mess.

My thoughts switch over to considering Evie's journal and trying to make an answer out of what little information I have. The journal isn't enough. The internet barely supplements it beyond the initial timeline of events. If only there were someone to tell us who told her how to lay the curse down on Benjamin.

What if I found a way to talk to Benjamin? He must still be out there in the woods.

The bad idea takes root as a real possible solution to all of this.

I can't go out looking for Benjamin. Not in this condition.

What would I do if I found him? Based off all the strange things that have happened here, I get the sense he doesn't care about being un-cursed. He seems to be enjoying his time out there fucking with anyone who comes within ten feet of this house.

I reach for my phone and decide to text Jonah.

> **Marisa:**
> I need to get out of this house. Nap isn't
> happening.

Only a few minutes pass before he responds.

> **Asshat:**
> Wobbly Leg? I have buckets for you from
> Hellie.

> **Marisa:**
> Yeah, sounds good. Meet there in an hour?

I check the clock on my phone for the first time all day, and my phone tells me it's only three thirty in the afternoon. Still, I don't send a follow up text suggesting we meet up later. If Jonah isn't game for early bird special at the dive bar, he'll say so.

He doesn't object, so I take another shower and get ready.

THE CAR WON'T START. THE FIRST FEW TIMES I TURN THE key in the ignition, the engine sputters like it might catch if I try again. When I try again, the smoke starts. It billows out of the hood in a thick black cloud that I don't dare mess with. It carries with it a chemical stench that stings my nose. Damn it.

I've known the car was ready to die for a long time, but I hoped it would hold on a bit longer. At least another month or so to give me time to get my life in order. That's not how the world works, though. Of course it died today, of all days.

Defeated, I text Jonah that I need a ride and he shows up not long after.

He finds me sitting on the front step and makes a face as he notices the remaining smoke in the air. Instead of commenting, he only nods in understanding.

"Thanks for picking me up," I say. "Sorry you had to come all the way back out."

"No need to apologize. We all hit our rough patches."

A flush of embarrassment rush through me. I don't have my life together, and it's already apparent to this guy who's only known me a few days.

"Can I repay you somehow? Let me buy drinks and snacks tonight. Please."

The sharp pressure of tears appears behind my eyes, but I blink it away. I refuse to cry right now. My entire body has a pulse, a violent aching rhythm that I can't dial down. All my insides feel like a too-loud club with bass booming, and I can't step outside myself to breathe. I'm trapped the way I used to be when someone dragged me out for drinks back in Madison, but this time there's no place to go.

"Marisa? You good?"

"I'm gonna pay tonight, okay?"

"Sure, whatever. What's going on? Do you need to talk?"

Behind me, bright green plastic catches my attention. The buckets for the horse Hellie said she'd send with Jonah. A distraction. Perfect.

"Are those the buckets Hellie's lending me? Let me bring them to the barn real quick."

Before he can answer or offer to help, my feet hit the stone path and I grab the buckets from the car, clutching them in both hands with white knuckles. It's possible I run from the driveway, as if I can escape any of this. I can't. Not permanently. Not unless I fix it. Right now, though, fixing anything seems miles outside my ability.

Even breathing seems outside my ability, as I sit on the barn floor next to a bag of grain. I hug my knees and suck in oxygen manually because my body has forgotten what to do. My lungs burn and my head swims. The ends of my fingers go numb and tingly. Is this a panic attack?

I squeeze my eyes shut and fight to calm down, but it only makes things spiral even more out of control. Stars erupt behind my pinched eyelids, and I curse myself for every decision I've ever made. Especially the ones that brought me to this moment of sitting on the dusty ground trying to breathe.

"Marisa?"

No. No. No. Go away, Jonah. You don't need to see me like this. I don't need your help.

Okay, that's a lie. Obviously I do, and not just for a ride to the bar. I won't say that out loud though.

"What's happening? Are you hurt?" The throbbing blood in my ears muffles his voice.

A warm pressure arrives on my shoulder, and I realize it's his hand. How long has it been since another human touched me to comfort me like this? I don't remember.

"I'm. Okay." A heavy, ragged breath punctuates each word.

"You can lean on me, if you want. I might be more comfortable than solid wood."

He doesn't say or ask anything else after his offer, and eventually I pull myself together enough to take him up on it. I lean against his flannel clad side, and he puts an arm around my shoulders. The warmth of him and the pressure of his embrace grounds me to this moment, and I find the normal rhythm of my breath after a long while of silence.

"You don't have to pay for dinner tonight," he says. "You don't owe me anything. This is what friends do."

I swallow hard against a lump in my throat. "Please. Let me pay for tonight. It's not enough, but it'll feel like something."

I can't put into reasonable words why this is so important to me. What I want to say is I want him to treat me like an equal, like a friend. I don't want to be a charity case or someone he keeps around because I'm so pathetic it makes him feel better about himself. All I want is to be a person to him, but I'm afraid I won't say the right thing. Worse, I'm afraid I'll be able to tell when he lies to me.

"Fine. You can foot the bill of beer and jalapeño poppers if you're going to keep being difficult."

"I'm not being difficult!" The audacity of this man, I swear.

"You are so. You can let people help you, you know. It's not a sign of weakness."

I cross my arms, annoyed that of course he makes a good point. What I didn't come here for was a voice of reason to combat every single toxic thought I let cross my mind about how I don't deserve help.

"So, are we going to go get jalapeño poppers or what?" I change the subject because I hate how clearly he at least sees me as something more complex than the sum of all my bullshit. "What the hell is a jalapeño popper anyway?"

Jonah feigns surprise with a gasp.

I roll my eyes.

"Jalapeño poppers are a classic bar food all over the country. They definitely have them in Wisconsin."

"Not the kind of places I used to go to, I can assure you."

"Well excuse me then, Miss Fancy," he teases.

"No, it was Mrs. Fancy. Now I'm Miss I-Will-Eat-Garbage-If-I-Have-To. I'm not picky. Now tell me what you're wasting my favor on."

Is this what it's like to have a normal friendship? The corners of my mouth rise to form a slight smile.

"Jalapeño peppers. Battered and deep fried and filled with cheese."

"Um. I take it back. I might be picky."

The back and forth with Jonah lifts my mood a little. Some of my stress evaporates and leaves room for a heavy exhaustion that takes up residence in my bones. For once though, I don't ache to go back inside and sleep. I actually want to go grab a beer and hang out with Jonah, because I might be able to feel like a normal girl in my mid twenties for a change.

TWENTY-ONE

THE WOBBLY LEG LOOKS DIFFERENT IN THE EVENING, which is when we end up arriving after my breakdown in the barn. With slightly dusty black and white checkered curtains pulled back from the tall glass windows, the place looks brighter than before. Less sketchy than my initial impression. In all fairness, I'd walked past and looked through the glass in the morning, which is no bar's prime. Now, with the early evening leading locals to upholstered stools for a cold drink to signal the end of another day, it feels lively.

Jonah picks a hightop by one of the windows over-looking the street. A string of holiday lights with tiny mason jars fixed to the bulbs hangs from the ceiling, and matching mason jars with electric tea candles sit in the center of each table. The rustic Pinterest style decor contrasts the scratched up wood floor and the tables with names and initials scratched into them, but somehow, just like at the diner, it works.

"Cute place," I say over criminally outdated country music.

Jonah twists his mouth to one side in thought as he glances around the space. "Cute, huh?"

"Yeah. I wasn't expecting it to be like this."

He shrugs. "Bowen's Leg has a few surprises for a town where nothing ever happens. We don't even have a parade on the Fourth of July anymore. And, to add insult to injury, we have an actual ordinance about throwing candy from vehicles."

"Yeah, that's called littering, my dude."

"It's not littering when it's a parade and there's people to catch the aforementioned candy!" He bangs his fists on the table, rattling the tea candles, but the grin on his face tells me he's messing around and not really angry about not being allowed to throw candy out his car window.

"Okay, fine. So why the ordinance?"

His expression goes serious, eyebrows furrowing slightly above darkened eyes. I wonder if he's still kidding.

"A kid got hit in the eye with a tootsie roll. Which, shit happens, but it was awful. You know how tootsie rolls reach a point where they could serve as ammunition in a pinch? This was one of those, and the lady on tootsie duty in the fire engine was whipping that shit at people. The damage to the eye was so bad, the kid almost had to have it removed."

"No way. Why do you think I'm this gullible?"

The corner of his mouth twitches. "I don't."

"Then why do you keep telling me these bullshit stories?"

"They're all true! Look, I'll find the story online."

He interrupts his search only to order jalapeño poppers

and a lager when the server comes. I order nachos and a pilsner, though the last traces of hangover still cling to me.

After a few minutes of searching, he turns his phone to me and shows me an article from 2006. I only read a paragraph before I push the device back at him.

"The kid didn't almost lose his eye," I say.

"Well, that's what everyone said."

"Everyone was making shit up."

"The rest of the story is true though. We have a real ordinance about candy throwing."

I still think Jonah's at least a little bit full of shit, but I let it go.

"Can you at least tell me why you keep helping me?" My own husband wouldn't have picked me up after my car broke down, he would've found a way to blame me for not having a more reliable vehicle like his shiny, leased Audi, but I don't add that part. I don't want to talk about Brent, and I definitely don't want Jonah to think I spend all my time making mental comparisons about the two.

"I told you. I'm very enthusiastic about being friends. Like, maybe too enthusiastic, but I haven't had anyone to just grab a beer with and hang. If I do go out, it's with work dudes and they're notably older than me and I can only talk about baseball for so long."

I hear Elise's voice in my head. This guy has to be a Gemini. She'd say that kind of shit about people, and I think she'd ask him his birthday right now and then declare something like "oh yeah, that makes sense," even if it didn't. Maybe when I get home I'll text her.

"Normally guys are enthusiastic about sex and that's it."

Jonah takes a long drink of his beer. "Rude. I guess I'm just not like other guys then."

"Ugh, who says that?"

"Not other guys, that's for sure."

This guy is ridiculous. The kind of ridiculous that comes from scrolling the not-so-bad parts of the internet and looking at memes no one will be able to translate in forty years without some kind of advanced degree. The same memes I have indexed away in my chronically online mental archives.

When our food arrives, Jonah holds out a jalapeño popper for me to try. It looks okay, I guess. Golden browned beer batter, barely a vegetable, cheese. I take it and blow on it to cool it down while it burns blisters onto the tips of my fingers.

Jonah cuts one of his in half with the edge of a fork, then pops a bite into his mouth. He covers his mouth with a hand and huffs out the heat collecting on his tongue, then sucks in cool air around the hot food.

"RIP your taste buds," I say.

He shakes his head and gives me a thumbs up despite glistening moisture in the corners of his eyes.

"That was very like other guys of you, you know."

His eyes widen and he swallows his mouthful of food. "How could you?"

The night goes on like this until I pay our tab and we head back outside to the car. I want to stay out longer, but the thought makes me a little bit uncomfortable. The idea feels a little like betraying myself, because I'm supposed to be figuring out what my new life is on my own.

We end up walking the length of downtown until we reach the tiny harbor, where only a few boats dot the expanse of sea.

"You have these stories about how tootsie rolls are illegal and about guys starting brawls in parking lots, but you still defend the town from anyone who tries to paint it in a bad light. Why? What makes you stay?" I ask.

"There's no one else to do it. Ever since Evie Ouellette

did whatever she did, the town lost something. Community programs lost funding. Tourism waned. People stopped caring about anything other than the legend, and then they stopped caring about that too. Everyone here is getting by, but nothing beyond that. The tourists live in their secluded camps on the outskirts, but they take their money out of town. Thirty years ago, we had a hundred miles or something of managed trails for every imaginable outdoor activity. Now they're all overgrown and, technically, closed to the public. Not like that stops anyone."

"What do you plan to do about it?"

"Start some kind of recreation group to sponsor activities. Get some funding to have a community center. Rebuild the trails and fishing areas and clean up the beaches so people actually want to use them, rather than leaving. Do my part to make this a place people want to be."

We stop at the edge of the boat launch, tips of our shoes mere inches from the water lapping up the oil-stained concrete. I want to know what it's like to have such a clear purpose in life. Since I started dating Brent, his goals became mine. My aspirations faded until I couldn't remember what they were.

Once I solve the mystery of what Evie did and where she went, what will I do then? Find a job somewhere, a new place to live. Then what? In this moment, not a single idea comes to mind.

"I wish I knew what I cared about as much as you care about fixing this place," I say.

He squeezes just above my elbow in a comforting gesture. "You don't have to know right now. Figure you out, then you can worry about what you want to do with your future."

We go quiet as we watch the water for a little longer, then head back up to where he parked across from the bar.

In the distance, some type of owl calls into the night. It's the first time I've heard a normal sound come from the darkness since I got here. Maybe there aren't any owls in the woods around my house because the presence of Evie and Benjamin drove them away.

Will I hear them when this is over?

CHAPTER

TWENTY-TWO

JONAH WAITS UNTIL I GET THE FRONT DOOR OPEN before he backs out of the driveway. I wave from the porch until he disappears down the road.

Beef's disgruntled meow from the corner of the kitchen where I keep his food reminds me I'm late and, because of my lateness, the cat is mere moments from a dramatic death by starvation.

I hurry into the house, shutting the door behind me, and take another step inside before I realize how wrong my surroundings feel. The thick scent of the forest after a heavy rain fills my nostrils, but it hasn't rained since I've been here.

Beef complains again.

When I take another step towards the wall with the light switch and key hook, my foot lands in something squishy and audibly damp.

"Did you puke, buddy?" I ask, though he doesn't vomit

134

often. What else could it be beneath my boot? A mouse maybe? Beef has killed a few, and every time their bodies are far more wet than they should be.

He meows in response, adding a rueful creak at the end to sell how miserable he is.

I hit the light and it illuminates the open space of the kitchen and living room. My heart sputters to a complete stop at the sight of the place.

The entire living room has been filled with mud, dried leaves, and sticks, like the forest floor has been swept inside by a tornado.

The keys in my hand clatter to the floor beside my dropped jaw.

It looks like a hurricane blew through the house, or like the place has been abandoned for years and nature started taking over. Barely a trace of the wood floor is visible beneath the mess, and only the armrests of the leather couch have been left untouched.

Beef sits atop the dresser where there once was strategically placed decor. Instead of whatever had been up there — candles, books? I don't remember — there's the cat beside a pile of wet leaves and the remains of a thin, black snake. He probably killed the snake, but he couldn't have done all of this. He's too small for this level of mayhem.

I let out a sick laugh. As if Beef's size is the one thing preventing him from turning the house into a compost pile.

This can't be possible. Even if someone's harassing me, they'd need a lot of free time and quite a few friends with wheelbarrows to accomplish this. Logic appears for a moment, then rushes away as I begin to comprehend the urgency of the situation.

Before panic fully seizes me, I manage to rush to the table beside the couch and check the drawer for Evie's journal. It's still there, untouched. I still have the one thing the other investigators didn't, not that it has helped me make any progress so far.

Okay, priorities. I don't get to be relieved about the journal because the entire living area is a mess and the sharp claws of anxiety have found my throat. With the flashlight on my phone, I search outside for footprints or wheelbarrow tracks leading to or from the house, but I find nothing. How could this happen? Who could do this?

I consider the idea that I forgot to lock the door when I left, and whoever did this locked them on the way out.

My head aches as I try remembering if I locked it or not, but my mind has purged everything from this morning except feeling most of the way dead.

I probably forgot.

God, I can't keep making these mistakes. I need to be better.

I have to clean this shit up.

Beef still perches on the dresser, and I rush to him to be sure he wasn't harmed throughout all of this. He sits, tense, at the edge of the wooden surface with his ears flat back and eyes wide, black voids. When I reach for him, he growls, then jumps down to run into the bedroom and hide under the bed.

He seems fine, then.

I raid the cabinet under the kitchen sink for cleaning supplies—black trash bags, paper towels, disinfectant wipes, and surface spray then do a walk around the house. The bedroom and bathroom both remain clean, as does the kitchen. Everything is centered right in the full view of the front door.

I start with the couch and dresser, cleaning methodically between the cushions and inside the drawers. Little bits of mud have collected in the thick, black seams of the couch and I clean them with an old toothbrush I found discarded in the far back of the bathroom cupboard. It takes two hours and two trash bags to clear off the furniture, and I still don't find any of the things that used to sit atop the dresser.

Wait. I should take a picture of this.

I open the camera app then frame the images so they contain as much of the damage as possible. Then I send them to Jonah because I don't know what else to do with them. The messages fail to send, though my phone says I'm connected to WiFi and have a perfect signal. They fail two more times before I give up. I have to get this out of here before it damages the floors.

With the litter scoop from Beef's box, I shovel away the heap of mud in the center of the floor. Upon further inspection, the pile is an entire ecosystem. Insects crawl alongside worms, centipedes, and more little snakes in a race to find the remains of half decomposed birds and rodents. Bones untouched, unbleached by the sun but stained and moistened by soil rise to the surface as I keep digging, and I try matching the sets. Tiny ribs and small, fragile skulls and the jaw of a rabbit or skunk wind up in a pile beside me, like I might reassemble them one night when I get lonely again.

I gag when I find something with flesh and matted fur still attached. It flies beyond the trash bag's opening when I fling it out of my hand, and it lands with a sickening sound.

The pile of bones I set aside crunch together when I grab them in both hands and throw them away. There is absolutely no reason why I should keep them. None. I need every trace of this out of the house.

My own bones creak when I stand to go pick up the half decayed creature I threw. Mud and who knows what else has soaked through and stained the knees of my jeans. There could even be blood on them.

No person or group of people did this. I know that,

despite reason begging me to search for a more palatable explanation.

So what do I do now? Finish Evie's journal? Go out into the woods and dig up whatever bodies are out there? Is that what Evie or Benjamin or whoever still lingers here wants? Closure?

Or do they want something more from me?

Everything they've done so far has happened around me, but they haven't hurt me. I wonder if they actually could, if they wanted to.

The thought makes my blood run cold.

TWENTY-THREE

I WAKE UP SLOUCHED OVER THE ARM OF THE COUCH clutching a balled up cotton blanket and with my neck bent at an unnatural angle. Everything from last night hangs over me like the fog of a barely remembered dream. It's all vivid flashes of images out of context, jolts of panic and fear, and the urgency of needing to react but being unable to move.

At some point during the night, Beef emerged from under the bed and now sits heavy against my shin, drawing attention to how I have my leg bent at the knee and the joint aches.

My phone battery has died and the screen has a smear of soil against it, gritty and real. A souvenir from last night to prove it wasn't a dream. I wish it had been, but even after I showered last night I still have half moons of dirt under my nails and the scent of the forest in my nostrils.

Beef has a slick streak of fur to one side of his mouth,

probably from the blood of the snake he killed. He doesn't let me near him with the paper towel I dampen to wash out the now crusted mess, so I leave him to figure it out on his own. Damn stubborn cat.

Without bothering to change out of sweatpants and an oversized t-shirt from, like, tenth grade, I pull on my boots and head outside. The bags of trash I left against the back bumper of the Toyota have vanished. Is there trash pick up around here? It doesn't seem likely, but it makes more sense than the bags being stolen.

Or they never existed.

No. Stop it.

I wish I could trust myself, but trust is a shaky thing. A newborn animal on quivering legs, unsure of itself and its surroundings but understanding it must stay close to the only thing it knows. My trust knows its limitations. It knows my memory doesn't hold onto things as well as it should. It knows someone else always has a better recollection of what really happened, because, really, what do I know?

I take another look around the driveway to check for the bags, which really have been taken or removed, then head down to the barn. The horse greets me the same way she usually does when I approach her stall. She nuzzles the pockets of my pants in search of treats, then goes to sulk in the back corner of her stall when she finds nothing. She digs at the ground with her front hoof and heaves out deep, meaningful sighs while I dump a portion of grain into her bucket. Each pellet hits the plastic with a smack and sounds almost like heavy rain in a way that's therapeutic.

"Did you see anything last night?" I ask her.

The crunching of tires from the gravel driveway snaps me out of my thoughts, and I turn too fast on my heels and lose my balance. My left elbow hits the wall hard and sends a violent tingling down my arm to my fingertips. My right arm scrapes down the plywood and probably catches half a dozen splinters in the places where the skin doesn't break.

The horse's head shoots up from her bucket and she turns, ears pricked forward, and stares at the driveway.

A familiar orange Subaru sits there and I lose what little energy I had. It isn't that I don't appreciate him, but I don't want to get too close to Jonah. At the rate we're going, a mistake feels inevitable and I can't deal with that right now. I don't know what I want. My singleness is too fresh, the old relationship an open wound that needs time to stitch itself back together.

I am getting way ahead of myself.

My primary concern should be that I am in my pajamas and half my hair defies the laws of gravity from where it pressed against my palm while I slept. I don't need to worry about the long con process of getting too close, of the risk of falling for someone. Presently, I need to worry about how much of a goblin I allow myself to be in front of him. The least I can do for myself is look like I have even a finger's grip of control over my life.

The sound of Jonah knocking on the front door echoes, muted, down to the barn. I comb my fingers through my hair and pull it into a messy bun, rub the crust from my eyes, and wipe the blood from my scraped elbow.

The horse stares at me, presumably judging me for getting all riled up and flustered over someone I don't need to impress. She snickers and bobs her head, then nudges against my stomach. Black horse hair remains stuck to my t-shirt when she goes back to nosing around in her bucket, and I pick some of it away before giving up.

Another series of knocks comes from the house, a bit firmer than before. I don't call up to tell him I'm down in the barn. If he comes down to find me here, I'll accept my fate, but if he chooses to leave and call later I won't be upset.

I sit on the lawnmower across from the stall with my feet up on the wheel and instinctively reach into my pockets for my phone. I'd forgotten I left it up in the house to charge. A quick glance around is all it takes for me to find something to occupy my time: a broom. I try purging the thoughts from my head—all of them—and focus entirely on cleaning the dust and hay and shavings from the barn's floor.

A mouse rushes out from behind the broom, plump from some treasure trove of food. It doesn't even startle me after everything. My only reaction is a monotone, "Oh hey, bro." It's the second one I've seen in here.

"Marisa?" Jonah calls from the entrance of the door I left open. "You in here?"

"Yep," I say, continuing to sweep.

He wears his usual flannel shirt, but today he has the sleeves rolled up because the temperature feels like spring. It seems people in Maine treat the first over forty degree day like we do in the midwest: like it's the first day of summer.

"What's up?" I ask. A nicer version of 'why are you here?'

"Uh, you sent me a bunch of pictures of your living room with no explanation last night, then didn't answer when I called and texted."

The pictures must have gone through sometime before my phone died, because I don't remember that happening.

He doesn't make it sound like there was anything wrong with the pictures, though.

I have a bad feeling.

"Oh. Was there anything weird about them?" I ask. "The pictures, not the lack of response."

He shakes his head. "I couldn't find anything, and I defi-nitely looked. I thought you were trying to tell me something."

My heart stops, and I fight the urge to sprint up to the house and check my phone to see what I sent.

"I was."

TWENTY-FOUR

My phone takes eight years to power back up. Or, at least, that's what it feels like.

The smudge of dirt on the screen remains, which I find unsettlingly comforting. There was dirt in here last night. The smudge is proof.

Jonah stands beside me next to the power outlet my phone's charger tethers us to. We huddle around the device like it is the only thing keeping us warm in an ice storm, waiting patiently for the illuminated logo to disappear and be replaced with my home screen.

"You can tell me what happened," he says.

"No. You won't believe me if you don't see it," I say. Right now, I'm losing grip on my belief in what I saw last night.

It doesn't matter that I felt the dirt on my hands, or the moisture through the knees of my jeans. Even without looking, I have a feeling the pants would show no signs of a mess.

When the phone finishes turning on, I tap the icon for messages and pull up the thread with Jonah. Each of the images I sent went through four times, and all of them are different from the images I meant to send last night. In them, the living room has no signs of mud. Not even an errant footprint from me tracking in mess on my boots.

"Fuck." I switch to my photo library, hoping for something different.

I don't find what I hoped for.

"This isn't right," I say. I can't even find it in me to be upset. Of course this happened. "These don't show what I saw last night."

My hands shake and lose grip on the device, and I let it tumble to the floor. The case will protect it. I don't care if it doesn't.

"What happened last night?"

I leave Jonah by the phone, and check between the cushions of the couch. Nothing hides inside, not like the dirt smeared across my phone, though two house centipedes lie dead beside the table. This place must be infested with the things. They're harmless, but looking at them makes me uneasy. With the toe of my boot, I kick them under the couch.

"I don't know. I thought ..."

I shouldn't say I thought I saw the living room full of mud, the couch piled high with filth. I should say I know I saw it.

"Marisa, you said you'd call the police if anything happened. That's what you agreed to when I said I'd help you."

"Yeah, what am I going to say?" I hold my hands out. "There's nothing here. Not a fucking thing."

Jonah recoils at the way I raise my voice.

I don't apologize.

"This room, right here where I'm standing was a mess. Not like someone came in and robbed the place, but like someone decided they were gonna dump a dozen truck loads of shit in the middle of my house. There was mud and sticks and—" I clench my fists. "There were little dead things. A snake, a bird. Little bones. Leaves."

I collapse onto the couch and pull my knees up to my chin.

"Jonah, I think I'm going crazy. The house was a complete mess last night and I cleaned it. I spent hours cleaning it, and I filled, like, six huge trash bags in the process. I left them outside to deal with in the morning, and they were gone when I went to feed the horse."

"You're not crazy," he says, not in a dismissive way.

"How else do you explain this then? The pictures on my phone don't show a mess. The trash bags are gone. The only thing left is a little dirt on my phone, and that could just as easily have come from my hand after I did something outside in the barn."

"I don't know," he admits. "That's what we're going to figure out."

Jonah takes a seat next to me, but instead of asking anymore questions, he lets me decompress.

He picks up Evie's journal, and reads while I stare forward at my reflection in the screen of the TV I haven't used since moving in. Under normal circumstances, I might've found comfort in curling up on the couch with a blanket and popcorn and a TV show I'd missed out on during the height of its popularity. That would have been more reasonable than what I've spent my time doing.

"What if it isn't a curse?" I say.

Jonah looks up. "What do you mean?"

"What if Evie figured out a way to give him eternal life so she could torture him longer?"

"That still sounds like a curse."

I think of what I've read so far, and, sure, Evie mentioned curses. She's mentioned a lot of things, but immortality's a common point of disagreement among people. Some think it would be great, because they could do everything they ever wanted. Other people believe it would terrible to watch everyone they care about die without them. It would probably also be terrible if your body were in constant pain.

"She mentioned clipping spruce trees for a ritual," I say, remembering the waypoints she described when she wrote about walking out to where Benjamin was trapped. "She also said his bones were poisoned."

"Spruce trees?" Jonah asks, picking up his cell phone and typing something. "I guess they're supposed to represent eternal life in some cultures. That would make sense, though they aren't toxic. Spruce is edible."

I take the journal and flip through the pages again. "I wonder if she left the other ingredients in the other entries."

The entries I already read only mention one other substance, and it's garlic extract. I add it to a list in the notes app of my phone along with the spruce. Then I go to where I left off after I learned Evie took Benjamin's fingers to prevent him from reversing the curse.

He can reach me, despite being miles into the woods. Not physically, but in spirit. He comes like the fog and takes my energy bit by bit. I should have taken him farther out. I could have brought him out of state, out of the country.

He's still stuck out there, but every day he takes another step to expand his territory.

"This is really messed up," Jonah says.

"Evie fucked up. Like, really fucked up."

There might have been a time where I might've seen similarities between Evie and myself. I might have wanted to take her side in all of this. I did, in the beginning, but I can't now. I've learned too much from her to still believe she'd been a good person and whatever happened had been a simple misunderstanding. She wasn't a hero. Benjamin may have killed Betty. He may have been an abuser or a cheat or any number of terrible things, but that doesn't make Evie's actions okay.

"I understand why the town hates her. I get why everyone extends that hate to her family," I say.

"They don't even know about the stuff in the journal. They only know—well, think—she did a murder and put down some curses and fled the consequences."

"What do I do with this information?" Who would believe me if I came forward and said Evie Ouellette took her friend's killer hostage, broke his bones, injected him with some kind of serum that poisoned his skeleton so his soul would be tied to it forever?

"Use it to undo what she did."

"All I know is the whole skeleton must be present to—" I look for her exact phrasing. "—cleanse him. I don't know what cleansing entails, and I don't know where the stolen fingers went."

God, I just said 'stolen fingers' in a perfectly serious, real life conversation.

TWENTY-FIVE

EVENTUALLY, JONAH HAS TO GO TO WORK. HE INSISTS IT would be okay if he called out so I wouldn't be alone, but I tell him I'll be fine. I need to be sure no one suspects he's hanging out here in this cursed place, though anyone driving by would see his atrocious car. Despite the concern about the Subaru, I cling to my hopes that I won't ruin his reputation and cause the town to turn on him. He wants to do things for this place to make it better, so, if someone goes down for fucking with Evie's shit, it's going to be me alone.

I decide to go outside and walk the horse in circles in the pasture to clear my head. Younger me would be psyched to know I had my own horse, and I embrace the opportunity to reconnect with a version of myself who enjoyed things.

The horse gets bored after a dozen or so laps and starts acting up. She nods her head up and down, teeth bared, while passing me. Then she decides to kick up clumps of dried grass in the infrequent instances where she has all four hooves on the ground.

"Can you cut it out, dude?" I say.

Everything I know about horses boils down to the fact that they read people's energy and adapt to it. My energy can't possibly suggest I have the patience for this behavior right now. Yet she still raises hell at the end of the lead no matter how sternly I demand she stop.

Feeling ballsy and a little curious in the bright afternoon daylight, I lead the horse out of her enclosure and decide to walk her along the trail that enters the woods. If she doesn't feel like walking in circles, fine, we'll walk through the creepy as hell, probably haunted forest instead. Maybe I will find something to lead me to Benjamin's remains.

The brush grows in thick despite still looking mostly dead and dormant from a long winter. The trail is barely a path between the trees, sometimes only wide enough for me to walk single file ahead of the horse. Other tracks weave around like a maze made by animals. At least, I hope they were made by animals.

All the horror movies I've ever seen come together in my head to create an alternate explanation for the paths. A cult of people who've left society behind in favor of nature, marching through these woods in search of food or water or something. Growing farther from the rest of humanity with each hour they spend separated. Conducting rituals, which probably aren't as dramatic and gruesome as the ones in movies, but look like that in my mind. Bloody, cannibalistic rituals with sharp blades and fire and screaming and living things turned to dead things in an instant.

I swear, I hear whispers in the distance, though I can't decipher the words.

A shiver crawls up my spine and I shake it off. There are no cannibals out here waiting to make me into sad girl jerky. Objectively, I'm the human equivalent of a chicken wing anyway at this point. I'd make a terribly unsatisfying meal for a group of forest cannibals.

Why am I like this?

Since the horse seems pleased with the change of scenery, I can focus more on my surroundings than on her. I search the forest floor for the usual signs of people — wrappers, trash, bottles, discarded clothes. Evie wouldn't have used these to mark a trail, because trash is easy to move and lose track of.

The whispers I thought I heard have quieted, but they linger among the silence. Someone is out here.

I need to find the truck she mentioned in her journal, or the tree with a U shaped trunk, or a copse of spruce trees. Benjamin lurks out here somewhere.

We go well past the mouth of the woods, and I lose track of time and direction. As long as I keep following the same path, I can turn around and walk back to the house without getting lost, right? I focus on making only the most subtle of turns to the left or right, and make note of waypoints. A fallen log with moss along the top, a stump covered in a dried family of mushrooms, a rock bigger than my dead car.

None of these things look like they've been visited by humans in a long time. They're too untouched, too wild.

In the quiet between the horse's steps is something heavy and unwelcome that doesn't belong among the serenity of the trees. I recognize the weight of the presence on my skin as the feeling of being watched I'd felt nearly every day since coming here. What is it? What else is out here?

The horse stops walking and won't budge when I tug the lead to draw her forward. Her eyes are frantic, with the whites showing as they dart around the forest in search of the thing she senses but can't find.

"It's okay," I tell her. She doesn't believe me, and won't allow me to pet her in an attempt to soothe her anxiety. "There is nothing out here. Just us."

Whatever part of me thinks lying to a horse will even work is the dumbest thing on the planet. She has senses and a prey instinct far stronger than anything possessed by a human, Earth's most dangerous yet unqualified predator. She knows better than me, so I step around her in the brush and begin leading her back the way we came.

Turning away from the place that unsettled her inspires her to move, but not quickly or without occasionally stopping in her tracks to check the area around us.

In the corner of my vision, I catch the edges of something pale moving through the trees. Was it human shaped or animal? I don't know. My brain couldn't make sense of anything beyond the color of it, or lack thereof, standing out against the earthy tones of the woods.

I turn in a full circle, searching for a trace of what I saw, then rub my eyes with the heels of my hands. A trick of the light. That's what it must have been. It was nothing more than the paranoia lingering on my skin like a slick of sweat. It moved too fast, too easily through the unkept nature to be a human, but what else could it be? A deer? Do mountain lions live out here?

Please let it be an animal, even one that could kill me in a fraction of a second. That would be better than whatever a person or their ghost might have in store for me.

The horse stares into the distance where I saw the apparition, and it takes a few solid tugs before she finally resumes walking again.

We keep going for a while longer before the wind picks up and I stop dead in the center of the path. The horse doesn't notice at first, and bumps her big head into my back before coming to a halt.

"Marisa ..."

My name appears like a breath, icy like a winter wind on the back of my neck. The hair on my skin stands on end, and I try to see as much as I can without turning my head, because what if there is something between the horse and me? With the hand not clutching her lead, I reach behind me and only find the horse's velvet muzzle.

It wasn't her breathing on me.

I don't know how I know that but I do.

"Marisa." The voice calls to me a bit firmer now, but it comes from a different direction than before.

Fuck.

The bony fingers of leafless trees say my name so quietly, it barely registers. Now that the thought has fully nested itself in my mind, I connect the voice to the one I know. The one belonging to someone I thought I could trust.

Jonah's voice comes from different directions in an uneven cadence and dread coils like a venomous snake in my chest.

It isn't him. It's a trick.

It has to be all in my head.

Jonah went to work. Jonah couldn't be bouncing around the forest like the voice is. Jonah wouldn't do this to me.

I thought I could trust him. I still think I can.

This is just another strange occurrence. Nothing more. Please let it be nothing.

As I try and pinpoint which direction the voice comes from, I spin until I get dizzy. The trees swirl around me, and the forest floor seems to dip out from beneath my feet.

"Shut up!" I yell. "Leave me alone."

The demand falls flat without adequate air in my lungs. I consider, only for a second, coming to a halt and stomping my feet into the ground as I scream for the voice—for Jonah's voice—to stop following me. To stop haunting me.

As I rush down the trail with the horse, I vaguely make note of features I remember passing in an attempt to convince myself we're going the right way. It doesn't matter, though, since my car won't start and the house isn't even safe now if whatever this is can get inside.

The horse and I slow when the whispers die down, and I pause at a little fork in the trail that I don't remember. I stare at it, looking for something I recognize to tell me which way to go because I didn't come out here for that Robert Frost bullshit about paths less traveled. I came out here, unintentionally at first, to find what's been hanging out around my house. Now that I have, I am scared and want to take the fastest path home regardless of how well traveled it is.

When I don't decide fast enough for her, the horse chooses the path for us. In doing so, she plants a foot directly on top of my flimsy boot. I yelp even before the pain kicks in and try to pull my foot away from her, but, alas, there is a thousand pound animal on it.

Tears collect in the corner of my eyes and, if I could, I would sit in the dirt and cry for as long as my body would allow.

I smack her on the shoulder twice before she realizes I want her to take a single step. When she does, all the blood rushes back to my foot and I bite my bottom lip against the wave of agony. I stand there for a minute until the pain fades into a vicious pulse, then I attempt a step. Another. I walk through the discomfort.

My foot can't be broken. I can't drive myself to the hospital. I can't afford to take the ambulance. And even if I still mostly believe Jonah is on my side, I can't shake the discomfort of hearing his voice surrounding me out here in the middle of nowhere.

CHAPTER

TWENTY-SIX

GETTING TO THE BARN AND LOCKING THE HORSE BACK UP in her stall happens somehow, though I couldn't pick out any of the details if anyone were to ask. How I wind up sitting in my underwear and t-shirt on the edge of the tub with my swollen foot submerged in warm water and Kosher salt—not Epsom, because I don't have that—, I couldn't tell you.

I have no memory of getting home.

My body crumples when I stop putting in effort to hold myself up, and I fold forward until I can't anymore.

The water fills the tub and it reaches halfway up my calves before I remember to turn it off. My head feels foggy. Every muscle in my body seems to have vanished, because I don't have any strength left in me.

I don't know what to think right now.

My skull is full of mud, preventing thought. I am so, so

156

tired, more so than I should be from being stepped on. However I got back here, it drained me mentally to the point where I can't even function.

With my aching foot submerged in the hot water, I swallow three of the painkillers Jonah brought the day I had a hangover. Was that only yesterday? Then I pick up my phone and dial Jonah's number. I can't tell the police, but I need to tell him what I heard.

The call goes straight to voicemail.

I try and fail three more times.

I slide off the edge of the tub and into the water, still in my clothes, and turn the faucet back on. My baggy shirt clings to my body as it soaks through, but I leave it on. The water washes over me, hot and salty and comforting. My foot throbs with its own pulse. Maybe now it's my only pulse. I haven't checked on my heart in a while, and it feels distant. Broken.

Separating real Jonah from the forest's impersonation of him is impossible, though I try. God, I try so hard. Even my recent memories of him from earlier today begin to warp into what I encountered in the woods. My brain rewrites everything I know about him until I feel skeptical.

Maybe I shouldn't have trusted him so quickly.

I wanted it so bad.

The warm water laps over me and I let the tub fill until all that sticks out is my face, then turn off the faucet. My ears fill and everything sounds a thousand miles away.

I stay like that for a while. Long enough that the pain in my foot begins to subside, along with my consciousness. I sink into a half sleep where the lines between dreams and reality blur.

Somewhere in the house, a door creaks open. My body twitches and sends a ripple through the bath, but I don't fully awaken because I never fell all the way asleep. I lie there, paralyzed, as other sounds follow the opening of the door.

Footsteps come into the house and grow louder as they approach the bedroom, careful and intentional, like the person walking means not to be heard.

I try to move, but my body refuses.

The steps come closer, past the doorframe and right up to the side of the tub. The scent of the forest floats in the air when they stop just out of view.

Didn't I lock the door?

If I could just turn my head, I could see who they are. From this angle, I only see the edge of a dark blur in my peripheral. I can't comprehend their height, their build. The figure stands, an unidentifiable shadow beside me.

"Who are you?" I ask, though the words don't emerge from my mouth as they should. They bounce around the room, seemingly originating from nothing. "Jonah?"

The swirling of my own voice around me makes my stomach turn sour. Bile climbs my throat and lingers at the back of my tongue, unable to force its way up and out. The tub rocks like a tiny boat in an angry sea, and the water inside sloshes violently with each wave the vessel strikes.

I tell myself I'm at the house. This is a dream. I can't drown on solid ground in the middle of the forest, miles from the ocean.

"Please don't hurt my cat."

Something lands in a clump in the water with a splash, then sinks down until it settles on my submerged chest. It begins to wriggle against my skin. Another, slightly heavier clump comes next. The feeling of worms like wet tendrils of hair crawls over me, I can't brush them away, can't tell my limbs to reach up and pluck them off me.

My body goes ice cold, and panic mixes with the nausea. The vomit in my throat chokes me, and my lungs burn.

"Why are you doing this?" How am I speaking if I'm not breathing?

The sound of metal against stone—a shovel against a rock in the soil—comes before my question dies in the air. It doesn't make sense. They couldn't dig through the hardwood floor. Yet another pile of what I now know is dirt lands on my cheek.

The shovelfuls of earth continue to bury me until it has no place else to go but in my mouth, my nostrils, my eyes.

I try and scream, to draw my voice back from where it ricochets against the walls and ceiling, but I've been suffocating for what feels like hours already.

The things that feast on death take over and begin the process of decomposition. My body is unwoven until first the skin has devoured, then the muscles, and finally the bones. It doesn't feel like being eaten alive. No, I think that would be excruciating. This is a warm humming in my body until the vibrations pull apart the cells that make me. This is returning home.

A crash comes from somewhere else in the house. The person who buried me, maybe? Or Beef knocking something over in a panic.

I fade into the buzzing feeling that my body is made of until consciousness wanes again. If I close my eyes, will I sleep or will I die?

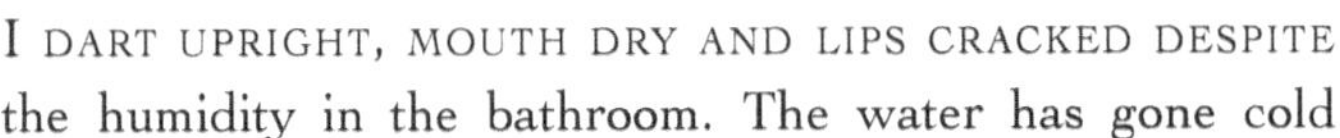

I DART UPRIGHT, MOUTH DRY AND LIPS CRACKED DESPITE the humidity in the bathroom. The water has gone cold around me, and my goosebumped body trembles in the bath. How long have I been here?

I glance around for any trace of whoever had been here, though now it feels like a dream.

Without any dirt on me, it had to have been a dream.

It felt so real, like I'd really been buried alive in the bathtub. But it wasn't real. It was an elaborate manifestation of my anxiety. The chemicals in my brain fell out of balance again and threw me into a spiral.

Again, I tell myself it wasn't real.

I say it aloud.

The tub drains with a rattling groan, and I peel off my soaked clothes and wrap myself in a towel. My foot hurts still, though not as bad, and I move sluggishly to the bedroom to dig a fresh pair of pajamas out of the suitcase I still haven't unpacked.

My hair hangs limp down my shoulders and reminds me of the weight of the worms tossed on me in the dream. I shudder, then tug it into a messy bun to keep it off my skin.

Dressed in warm pajamas, I sit on the edge of the bed and listen to my teeth chatter from sitting in the cold bath for who knows how long. My nose itches as if the spring pollen that knocks me down every year has come out early, and I rub at it with my hand.

The itching doesn't let up, so I rise again to grab a square of toilet paper from the bathroom and blow my nose. The effort makes my head spin, like I've blown too hard, but I force the air out with enough force to shake loose whatever causes the tickling.

I toss the balled up toilet paper into the trash bin, then notice myself in the mirror. Beneath my left nostril, a smear of dark brown stands out against my pale skin.

My fingertips meet the smear, and it's coarse. Coarse like dirt.

I look over at the tub as I wipe my nose again, and a thick trail of mud runs down the center of the white acrylic.

CHAPTER

TWENTY-SEVEN

My entire body tingles with numbness as I scrub the dirt from the bottom of the tub. The smell of the cleaner I sprayed on the mess stings my nose. A stain remains, no matter how hard I scrub with a coarse sponge. What I saw disconnects from what I see now, like the discoloration of the white tub could be from age and not a nightmare.

Wait.

My chest seizes in panic.

Where the hell is Beef? Is he okay?

I drop the sponge and discard the spray bottle of cleaner on the lip of the tub, then rush out of the bathroom. From the bedroom window, I see the sky glowing with sunrise or sunset but I don't know which. Beef should have come for me long ago. He would have started kneading my clothes with his claws, hard enough to press the sharp tips of them into my skin without drawing blood.

He isn't in the bedroom—not atop my bed nor hiding underneath it. I pull open the small closet door, but only empty space greets me. He'd be easy to spot in here, because the only things in here are a few hangers on the rack.

I try the living room next, searching under the couch and between the cushions and behind all the pieces of furniture pressed against walls.

Shit.

The tinkling of kibble dropping into his bowl should draw him out, but it doesn't. The usually mild smell of hard chunks of ambiguous seafood makes my stomach twist, and I gag.

Shit.

Shit. Shit. Shit.

Could he have gotten outside?

"Beef! Where are you?" I call. "Here, kitty."

Silence greets me in response. No pitter patter of his cute little feet. No crashing of small objects as he frees himself from whatever nook he wedged himself into. Not even a meow to let me know he heard the food and that he's stuck or something.

I return to my bedroom and tear the sheets off the mattress and the cases off the pillows, as if he could be hiding inside without me noticing. Next, I pull the mattress off the box spring, and flip the box spring over to check for places he could be.

My foot aches, and I lower myself to the ground atop a heap of sheets and blankets. No Beef. I look down at my hands and try and slow my breathing and loosen the grip of terror clutching my chest.

One more lap around the house, then I have to go outside and search.

First, I stop at the fridge in a single moment of clarity

among the madness in my head and pinch a bite sized piece of provolone cheese off a slice in the packet.

"Beef, buddy. I have special cheese," I call. "Your favorite special cheese."

If he doesn't come for the provolone, he's probably dead.

No.

I squeeze my eyes shut against the intrusion. My cat is not dead. He is somewhere. I will find him.

He will come out for cheese.

He will.

I hold the shred of cheese in my open palm like a precious, delicate thing and go through the house in the opposite direction from the first time. This time, I notice the door to the second bedroom hangs open a sliver. Easy enough to miss if I assumed it were still locked like it's been the whole time I've been here.

When I nudge the door the rest of the way, I stare into a normal room with a wooden dresser and a twin bed covered in a floral comforter. Against one wall, a stack of antique frames lean with the pictures facing inward. Each one has a couple lines of neat script on the cardboard back. A couple plastic totes with a layer of dust on the top sit stacked in the corner with a strip of tape to mark the contents. Nothing remarkable, really. Winter clothes and holiday decorations that had been put away a long time ago.

The deepest, bottom drawer of the dresser gapes open and its contents appears to have been disturbed by the way it sticks out. A pale gray knit blanket spills over the front of the drawer like someone had pulled it out, and a lime green and yellow quilt has been pushed to one side.

Something small and white stands out against the dark wood bottom of the drawer. A small stone, maybe. No, it's narrow and only a little over an inch long.

Oh.

I reach down to take the object, but a low growl rumbles from inside the drawer.

My hand whips back and I yelp. When I glance down into a burrow made in the blankets, I find two reflective eyes staring back at me. Beef hisses before he realizes it's only me, then attempts to squirm out of the nest he made. Once out, he paws at the hand I've closed around the piece of cheese I brought for him.

I breathe and scratch between Beef's ears, but he shies away from the attention as soon as the cheese is gone. He looks at the drawer and hisses again, then sulks out of the room.

Again, I reach into the drawer and, this time, I retrieve the white object. I pull out all the blankets from the drawer and shake them out until I have six little bones. The flesh has been removed and they have been bleached, but I know who they belong to.

Beef found the missing pieces of Benjamin's skeleton. The thing we need to send the man away for good.

I inspect them carefully, suddenly afraid I might break them. Where is the safest place to put them?

When I stand, I see Beef peering around the doorframe with wide eyes. I don't know what's going on with him. I don't know what's going on with anything, really.

I close the door behind me, double-checking to be sure it clicks shut.

In the kitchen, I wrap the bones in a paper towel, then place the bundle in a plastic bag and stick it at the back of a drawer where no one will think to look for them.

TWENTY-EIGHT

"Hey Jonah. It's me, Marisa. Um, I'm not sure what's going on, but I'm a little worried. Can you call me when you get a chance? Please."

By the time I cave and leave a voicemail for Jonah, I've lost track of how many times I tried calling. It stops going straight to voicemail at some point, which at first made me feel hopeful. His phone is back on. That's good.

He still doesn't answer my calls.

I have the sinking feeling something is wrong. Either he's ignoring me or he's hurt. Maybe even worse than hurt.

Keys in hand, I go outside and try starting my dead Toyota. If only it would start, I could check the farm and garden store and see if Jonah is working. I could try and find Hellie and Jack's number to see if they've heard anything.

The engine clicks three times before it chokes.

Guess I won't be going anywhere.

When my phone erupts into the default ringtone set to top volume, I practically dive for the device. It's Jonah, finally calling me back. I know it. It wouldn't be anyone else.

I don't even look at the screen when I answer the call and press the phone to my ear.

"I've been waiting to hear back from you for two days. Where have you—"

The voice on the other end cuts me off. Not Jonah.

Brent.

"It's been a little while. Wanted to check and see if you've gotten a job yet and can transfer me some money for the water heater."

I clench my teeth so hard, a little muscle in my jaw twitches. The words linger within reach. Fuck off Brent. Fuck off Brent. Fuck. Off. Brent. At the tip of my tongue. Right behind my teeth. If I were stronger, I would say them. Hurl them at him like grenades and burn down the last bridge leading him to me.

"Not yet. S—" I stop myself with the heel of my hand in my mouth. I will not apologize.

"If you can't find a job where you are, you should go somewhere else where there's a better hiring market. Did you do any research before you left?"

"How exactly do you think I would have done that?" I snap just a little. "With all the notice you gave? What, two days of researching the best places to move after your husband decides your marriage is done and he wants you out? You have to be kidding me."

My tongue burns. I want my words to scald him and leave angry, red blisters on his skin.

But they probably don't, and that makes everything worse.

Brent scoffs. "Typical. You really should have had a contingency plan."

"Oh fuck off." There it is. "Nobody plans for their husband to be a sack of shit."

"It's not my fault you weren't satisfied with the life I gave you. You didn't need to worry about money or work or anything. All you had to do was be a good partner."

"You know what, Brent. No. I'm not listening to this. I'm done. We're done. I didn't want to be some mindless cheerleader for you. You wanted that, and you tried making me into it. You wouldn't know partnership if it cut off your dick and slapped you with it."

"Whatever, Marisa. Once we sort out the water heater, you can delete my number if that's what you think will help you move on."

The audacity—the fucking audacity—of this man to make it seem like I'm the one putting him out by having this conversation. Of course he spun the argument to position himself as the victim and me the villain. I know the story by heart now. The familiarity of his tired narrative shouldn't make me angry anymore, but it does. It makes me livid.

"You're the one who called me. You could have left me the fuck alone like you were so good at before. Why can't you do that now? Why do you need me now? I know you have enough money to fix the thing yourself. So what do you want?"

He sighs deeply into the phone, and I envision him fidgeting with a paperclip or something until its form becomes unrecognizable. "You lived here too. Half the damage is yours, so it's only fair you pay for it."

"I'm not doing this right now."

I hang up on him before he can say anything else, then go to block his number again. It's already blocked. The option beneath the number only gives me the option to unblock the caller.

What the hell?

My entire body shakes from the adrenaline of telling him off. It should feel like a win. Anyone else might feel victorious for telling their jerk ex-husband off and leaving him hanging with an expensive bill for some bullshit that is fully his problem, but I don't.

He landed some hits that threw me back in time to when I believed I was broken, that I was the one shutting myself out, closing myself off to anything outside my house, and he was doing everything to help me back up. He really does know how to make a girl feel ungrateful.

But I am not ungrateful. I'm not perfect, but I'm not the monster he wants me to think I am.

How did I not see how toxic he was sooner? What did I even see in him, if this is what he's really like?

Pissed, I slam the car door shut and storm back into the house. I don't bother trying to call Jonah again. The anger from Brent's comments infects all of me, until I'm mad at Jonah for abandoning me without saying anything. He told me he'd help. He told me I shouldn't be alone. So where is he? Not here. Not fucking helping me.

"Fuck that guy, right B?" I ask the cat, who looks at me with a face like the moon when I reenter the house.

I imagine him affirming me in some way, even though he simply blinks once then resumes his very good impression of a large and round hunk of rock.

I take out Evie's journal, depending on her words to calm me down. There isn't anything particularly cathartic about her entries, but she writes about such extreme acts that it makes me feel better about myself. If nothing else, at least I have no intention of killing or placing a curse on either of the men I want to smack.

Betty visited me today.

I haven't seen her in such a long, long time. She looked beautiful like the day I met her, and I kissed her even though Roger was in the room with me. I missed her so much. I thought Benjamin killed her.

Roger didn't say a word to her the entire time we sat together. Men get so jealous over the silliest things.

Betty told me I saved her from Benjamin. She told me he was violent and that he'd hurt her.

My jaw drops. I wasn't expecting this.

"I thought Betty died," I say to the cat. He doesn't know what I'm talking about, but it beats talking to myself.

Before I move on to the next page, I rise to get another cup of coffee. The caffeine doesn't affect me anymore, but I still drink it out of habit. I've gotten used to drinking it while I read this thing.

The next entry contradicts the one I read before my coffee. Evie's handwriting remains messy and disorganized through both of today's entries, but this one feels so much angrier. Now it looks like she held the pen in her fist, drawing hard, angry lines to complete the words. In places, the pen tore through the paper.

We returned to Benjamin's altar. Betty was covered in blood. She told me she didn't want me to see her like that, but she was covered in it. She had a gash on her head along her hairline, and one of her eyes was full of blood. The opposite eye was circled in deep, black bruises.

She didn't move right. I thought her leg was broken, but it was all of her. Her back, her ribs, her arms.

She should never have left me. This would never have happened if she stayed.

CHAPTER

TWENTY-NINE

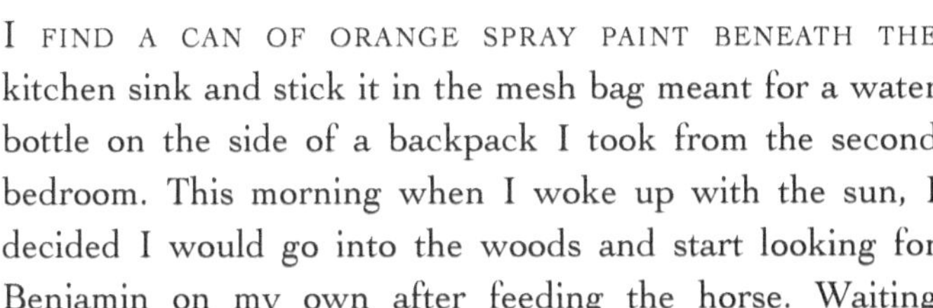

I FIND A CAN OF ORANGE SPRAY PAINT BENEATH THE kitchen sink and stick it in the mesh bag meant for a water bottle on the side of a backpack I took from the second bedroom. This morning when I woke up with the sun, I decided I would go into the woods and start looking for Benjamin on my own after feeding the horse. Waiting around for Jonah to call me back has gotten old after three days. I guess he's done with this.

The hurt has been replaced with embarrassment and frustration. He could have at least told me he was backing out.

Outside, the weather is a bit warmer than it has been, but a misty rain bites at my cheeks. I tug the hood of my sweatshirt up over my ears and zip my coat for added insulation.

In the woods, I mark my trail by spraying orange circles on trees as I pass. Way in the back of my mind, I wonder if

171

the marks will end up distorted, bending reality like the photos I took of the horse or the mess in the house. If I get lost out here, what happens then? Jonah won't answer, so that leaves calling 911 as the only option. Great.

Nothing strange has happened yet this morning, or at all since the incident in the bathtub. I let myself believe that means today might be close to normal.

I think about the last two pages of Evie's journal. One where she saw her friend, healthy and safe, and another where she saw her friend beaten and bloody. They had to be hallucinations, both of them.

Since I've been seeing things that aren't there, I can't blame myself anymore. Benjamin, or whoever haunts this place, must be able to make the inhabitants see things. He made me see a living room full of mud. Beyond that, he tricked me into thinking I felt the cool, damp soil on my hands. Then, in the tub, he tricked my brain into thinking my skin felt the pressure of being buried alive.

He made me hear Jonah's voice in the woods.

It could explain why Jonah has been absent. Maybe the same thing happened to him, and maybe he was too afraid to come back out and face the monster after.

I wouldn't blame him.

Or the voice really did belong to Jonah, and he's been inaccessible now that I've figured out his role in all of this.

The forest lies dormant still, though the end of winter approaches. The ground hasn't seen snow in a while, but hasn't quite awakened yet. In the trees that bear their last clingy, browned leaves, a few little birds sing. Aside from that and the sound of my boots crunching sticks and leaves, I hear no other sounds. No Jonah.

First, I go straight west into the forest, following the compass app on my phone to be sure I stay on track. I wander for hours without finding anything before I turn back and try another direction. If I have to scope out the entire forest, it's going to be a long time before I find what I need.

According to my phone, I've walked almost a mile northwest before I find a sign that I'm on the right track. A white, plastic bag has been tied around a tree branch. The material is tattered and torn, but not decayed. It still has a long time left before that happens. Evie mentioned it in her journal, but it could as easily be from her as it could be from someone else.

I spray another circle on the tree with the bag, then keep moving.

An uneasy feeling creeps over me, and I wish I hadn't come out here alone without the five iron. The nerves at the surface of my skin recall the sensation of dirt being tossed on top of me. I brush the feeling off, or try to, but it remains.

Whatever I thought about Elise's stories of the house being haunted or there having been a murder committed here, I never would have guessed this is where I'd be. Even when I decided to read the journal and figure out what happened, to stop the weird events Benjamin caused, I didn't think it would be this bad.

I didn't know things like this were real.

Between two trees up ahead, I see the red, rusted metal of an antique car, partially obscured by a little evergreen. Another of the waypoints Evie mentioned.

Except, I thought I remember her saying she passed a truck. The vehicle before me is a car, not a truck. The rusted out hood has been propped open and the machinery inside contains hundreds of acorns. It had been a good place for a squirrel to hide their food for the winter.

Could there be two old, rusty vehicles out here? It

wouldn't be unreasonable to think someone dumped their junk out here.

Regardless, northwest seems like a promising direction. I'd go further today, but my legs ache from trudging along out here on nothing more than two pieces of toast and three cups of coffee. My body definitely needs food and water right now. I'd also prefer not to be out here when it starts getting dark, so I leave a bright orange X painted on the last tree I pass, a thick trunked behemoth grown right beside the abandoned car.

I ARRIVE HOME TO FIND A FAMILIAR ORANGE SUBARU IN my driveway. Despite the chill in the air, sweat weighs my hair down and leaves it looking stringy and gross. I probably have dirt on my face and under my nails along with the spray paint on the tip of the finger I used to depress the nozzle.

"Where have you been?" Jonah rushes to me, and I have no idea why he's here and what makes him think I have to answer to him after he's ghosted me—ha, ghost— for three days. "I thought we were going to Wobbly Leg tonight. You said you wanted mozzarella sticks."

Now that he mentions them, I could go for some mozzarella sticks. I don't say that though, because I can't say anything through my confusion.

"I was worried sick," he continues.

"Um. What the hell is going on right now?" I say.

"No, that's what I'm asking you. Where were you?" he demands. "Have you been out there all weekend?"

"No. I haven't heard from you in three days. I tried to call you. I needed you." I want so badly to tell him about the incident in the bath, but I can't make myself do it. Even just thinking about it makes me feel claustrophobic now. "So I figured you were done with this, so I went looking for Benjamin's body, altar, whatever by myself."

The intensity held solely in his eyebrows lessens, and his features go slack. I don't like the way his expression changes at once from frustration to something worse: confusion.

"We talked yesterday and the day before," he says. "Face to face. The day before you said you dropped your phone in the sink and broke it. Yesterday you told me you didn't feel well, but we made plans to get drinks and snacks today."

Jonah doesn't know about the things Benjamin can do, but I think they extend beyond me. He made up conversations between Jonah and me that didn't happen. Did he also trick me into thinking I'd called and called, with no answer?

"We didn't have that conversation. We haven't talked since the day we started listing off things Evie might have put in a potion."

"What does that mean?"

I tell him what it means, in no uncertain terms. My phone never fell in the sink. Jonah and I never made plans to meet up tonight. He didn't interact with me at all for three days, though he showed up and attempted to reach me. Benjamin fabricated all of it. He can do whatever he wants to us, as long as we stay within his reach.

"I think, if you hadn't come to check on me, he wouldn't have gotten to you. This is his place. He can only reach us here, give or take a few feet."

Evie said in the journal that Benjamin had been stuck to wander a small portion of land. The house must be included in that. So what does that give him? A couple miles in any direction from his bones? Compared to how much freedom

Jonah and I have to leave the property, a few miles seems like nothing. He must be miserable, exactly like Evie wanted.

I wonder if she found herself miserable too, after everything.

No matter what, I'm going to figure this out. This is what I came here for, even if I didn't know it until today.

I wasn't the one to tell Brent to leave. He decided on his own that I couldn't live up to his expectations, so he replaced me. I didn't even get to take control of my new living situation either.

This time, I'll be the one to choose how things end.

CHAPTER

THIRTY

THE NEXT DAY, JONAH BRINGS ME TO SUNDAY DINNER with Hellie and Jack, because the bar isn't open on Sundays and the three of them agree I should have a home cooked meal. Jack insists it will make me feel invincible. I don't believe him. At this point, it would take a miracle to make me feel even the slightest bit of confidence, but getting out of the house and being around people where Benjamin can't torment me sounds pretty great.

Jonah picks me up, and we ride in mostly exhausted silence. Despite knowing Benjamin created the rift between us, a lingering weirdness remains. We don't talk about it, though. I assume it'll fade, and it doesn't feel right talking about Benjamin and Evie and their mischief while we're outside their reach. Today, we can pretend to be two normal people doing normal things.

I can't even envision what my life looks like when this all ends. Do I have a future here in Bowen's Leg, or do I leave as soon as I finish my task? I don't know what I want to do next. Beyond promising myself I'll be the one to decide my fate, I haven't given it much thought, really.

Jonah turns down a narrow dirt driveway with a red barn and historic looking white house about half a mile down. By the barn, a large pasture sprawls across the yard. Two horses gather around a pile of hay. In a separate area, three donkeys too small to comprehend chase one another around. A chicken coop, also barn red with white trim, sits beside the house and a small flock of hens wander freely in the dried grass searching for bugs.

This is the place of my dreams, and I allow myself to fantasize for a minute about what it would be like to live in a home like this.

We climb out of the car and head up a tidy stone path leading to the house. When I see the front door swing open and a familiar tall woman with graying hair in a messy ponytail emerges with the brown and white pitbulls at her side, I plant myself back in the present.

"Hi! It's great to see you again, Marisa," she says. The dogs sit politely beside her, looking at me as if wondering whether I brought treats. "Dinner is about ready. Jack's out back, I think."

Jonah laughs. "Waxing the tractor again?"

Hellie rolls her eyes good-naturedly. "He got that out of the way this morning so he could dedicate his undivided attention to the smoker."

As they catch up, I take in as much of the surrounding area as I can. I want to keep this place close.

"It's beautiful here," I say. "You and Jack do this all yourself?"

"Jonah helps when he can. He's useless with the horses though," Hellie says.

He nods instead of defending himself.

"I wanted to ask you if you'd be interested in farm sitting for us occasionally. Our previous caretaker moved south, and we need someone who knows horses."

I blink.

"We'll pay you, obviously."

"I could do that," I say. "I need to get my car fixed before I'm mobile again, but sure. Sign me up."

"Great. Let me show you around and introduce you to everyone."

"If Duchess likes you, consider yourself a goddess," Jonah says. "She's the absolute worst animal I've ever met."

Hellie fake gasps. "Duchess is simply misunderstood and can tell you don't like her."

I don't ask because it seems like another inside joke between the two of them.

Hellie claps her hands once and the dogs rise, and then trot in the direction of the barn.

Inside, she shows me all the grain bins and dry erase boards with which animal gets which food at which time and in which quantity. The notes get as detailed as saying which of the donkeys and horses can have peppermint treats, and which ones prefer oat treats. Holy shit, this woman. I need her to make a dry erase board for me to get my damn life together.

Outside, each animal has a halter of a different color with a metal engraved name tag on one side. She introduces me to the donkeys first. The three of them are all gray and fluffy and so small.

"These are Stumble, Ricky, and Majesty." She reaches out to scratch Stumble's furry forehead. "They stay separate from the horses because Ricky is an ass—" she laughs again from the bottom of her stomach. "A literal ass! Anyway, he tries to bite the hell out of the horses and then they kick him. It never ends well."

"Okay." I should say something more so I seem competent, but I can't. I am incredibly overwhelmed by this woman. She is terrifying in a way that I want to be when I grow up but also I know I could never pull it off. She's glamorous in this I don't give a single shit about my appearance kind of way. Meanwhile, I too don't give a shit about my appearance and it doesn't quite work like it does for her.

We leave the donkeys after Hellie feeds them treats from the pockets of her jeans. The dogs run full speed around the pasture with one of the donkeys—Majesty?— and I could stand here and watch them go all day.

Next, Hellie takes me and Jonah to the other pasture where the two horses, one chestnut and one a dappled gray, swish their tails, unbothered by our arrival

"That's Duchess. The brown one. She's mean."

"Take it back," Hellie demands. "She likes you and you hurt her feelings when you don't pet her."

"She charges at me."

"You would know it if she really charged, which she doesn't. She approaches you because she wants you to pet her, and you get frightened." Hellie turns from Jonah to me. "This is why we need a caretaker for the animals. Jonah's never been comfortable with them."

I look over at him, and he shrugs.

"Since Jonah has informed you of Duchess, the other horse is Crabapple." Hellie drops two baby carrots in my palm. "Why don't you introduce yourself."

If I weren't already aware of Jonah's discomfort around horses, I might take his opinions on Duchess more seriously. But he's even skittish around Beef, so I stick my hand out with a flat palm and offer one of the carrots to each horse. The soft velvet of their muzzles tickles my palm, then they go back to wandering the pasture when they've realized I only had the two treats.

Hellie gives me a thumbs up—a good sign, I think—then we head towards the chickens.

She rattles off their names, but they don't stick in my memory—except I'm pretty sure I heard one is named Danielle. In the light breeze, I catch the scent of something smoky cooking from behind the house. Whatever Jack has prepared lures my appetite out of hiding. My mouth might literally be watering like a cartoon character, though I'd have to see my reflection to confirm the suspicion.

Finally, we climb the slight hill back to the house and Hellie leads us to a screened in porch off the rear of the building. The pristine, white table has been set with white and navy checked napkins, silver cutlery, and a pitcher of water with glasses ready to be filled. A chiminea sits on one side of the space, pushing heat towards the table to chase away the lingering chill.

She tells us to take a seat. I do, but Jonah wanders back into the house and returns trailing her. They each carry something—Hellie a wooden bowl covered with a cloth towel and a dish of butter, and Jonah a blue cooler I assume contains drinks.

He proves me right when he sets it down and removes four cans, then sets one at each table setting.

"You want beer?" he asks as he sets my can down.

"Sure."

"Good. Jack's making brisket, and he insists this beer is the perfect companion. He's not wrong. It's good. But I don't know enough about pairing things with other things to know if he's right. I'm not sure he knows either, and just likes the combination himself."

Hellie laughs at that, and Jack enters right in time to ask what everyone thinks is so funny.

Dinner continues like this, with lighthearted jokes that have nothing to do with ghosts, curses, or monsters. I eat more brisket and cole slaw than I knew was possible, and let myself enjoy the night. I'll deal with everything in the morning.

Tonight, I get to feel like I belong somewhere for the first time in a long time, even if I don't.

CHAPTER

THIRTY-ONE

"So, uh. I heard your voice in the woods," I say on the drive back to my house. "A couple days ago."

In the glow from the dashboard, I see Jonah look at me. "You what?"

"I went for a walk in the woods to see if I could find some of the waypoints Evie mentioned being on the way to where she left Benjamin. I heard your voice while I was out there. You were at work. I know that. I'm not saying I thought it was you, but it *was* your voice."

Jonah considers this for a long moment.

"You went out there alone?" he asks. I thought he already knew, based on how he arrived at my house to find me returning from within the trees.

"Well, no. I took the horse."

"Marisa, that's not—" His voice is strained, like the words want to come out louder and angrier than they do. "What the hell were you thinking?"

"I thought I might be able to find something without making you go out there."

"Did you?"

"Kind of. I tagged the trees with spray paint so I could find my way back."

"That ... that's smart. Good idea." He makes the turn into my driveway and parks. Neither of us move to get out after he puts the Subaru in park. "The paint. The rest was a bad idea."

I unbuckle my seatbelt, but remain in the car. It would be easy to leave, to go inside and avoid the rest of this conversation, but I can't risk losing Jonah for another couple of days—or even longer. "Yeah. Not my brightest, but I couldn't wait any longer and I thought ... Benjamin made me think you were ignoring my calls."

"Next time you go out, we go together. Okay?"

We make plans to meet up in the morning and go out to follow the path I started. I tell him about the white plastic bag and the old car, forgetting for a moment about the voice and the other things Benjamin made me experience. The realization of how deep a pile of shit I've found myself in hits me then, and it hits me hard.

Have I been in denial this whole time? How could I not be scared off my ass after everything?

What is wrong with me?

"This is really bad, isn't it?" I say. "He made you think we had a whole conversation. He made me think I was calling you and getting only voicemail. What if you hadn't come when I was around yesterday? Would you have even known if I was dead? How long would it have taken?"

Oh no. I feel myself tipping into the spiral.

And then I drop.

All of it sinks in, heavy and toxic and deadly. Benjamin

could have killed me, and nobody would have thought to look for me. He still could.

"Would it give you the wrong idea if I asked you not to leave?" I ask. "Because I don't want to give you the wrong idea. I'm not ... in a place where I'm ready for that. But I realized now that, even thought I thought he couldn't hurt me, I think he can and I need your help. Ever since he made me hear your voice out there, I've been having a hard time. I don't know if I can trust myself, but I think I can trust you."

I run out of breath before I run out of words, and I inhale hard when my lungs finally refuse to push another syllable past my lips.

What if he says no? I don't have anyone else to ask, and I don't have anywhere else to go. Undoing Evie's mess alone feels impossible now, and I can't imagine doing it without him. It's too big, and we've come too far.

"I've been hoping you'd ask. I have an overnight bag in the trunk."

The statement stops me short.

"Excuse me?"

"I like to be ready."

"For what?"

"Platonic sleepovers in aggressively haunted houses, obviously," he jokes. "Seriously though, I don't expect anything. That's not why I'm here. I've told you that."

"Thank you." It comes out as barely a whisper.

We're going to do this. We're going to solve the mystery of What The Fuck Is Going On At Marisa's House once and for all. We're going to stop a curse. Then Jonah can go rebuild the community and make the town what it deserves to be, without the stain of Evie's misdeeds to ruin it.

Jonah grabs his overnight bag, which looks far larger than a bag intended for a single night. I don't question it.

Inside, the lamp by the couch emits a warm glow and casts the house in light. I'd left it on so I wouldn't have to come back to shadows.

Before I set off in search of blankets and a pillow for Jonah, I check the drawer in the kitchen where I put Benjamin's missing bones. The bag remains where I left it, but I open it and check inside the folded paper towel to be sure all of them are present. Once I know they haven't been moved, I tuck them back away.

"Are those ... are those bones?" Jonah asks. I didn't know he was behind me.

"Finger bones." I don't actually know that for certain, but they look like the segments of a finger and I hope the only bones in here are the ones we need. You know, our skeletons, Beef's skeleton, and the finger bones Evie took from Benjamin. I ask the universe politely to not put any additional bones in my path for a while. "The ones she took."

"Where did you find them?"

I glance over at Beef, who has found a centipede and bats it with his paw. What is it with this place and centipedes?

"Beef found them in a drawer while he was crawling around causing problems."

The cat descends onto the centipede's body with his teeth, then meows to declare his intent to remove each of the bug's thirty-ish legs. I haven't seen Beef move like this, well, ever. Before, he didn't seem to care about playing or hunting. Maybe centipedes are delicious. That would explain his interest.

"That's ... unsettling."

"Don't tell me you're afraid of cats too," I groan.

"No. No, of course not. I'm only afraid of your cat. He

hates me and I'm half convinced he plans to sit on my neck tonight and suffocate me. You've seen how he glares at me."

"That's just his face! He has resting murder face!"

Beef looks up at us, unimpressed by the noise. The back half—or maybe it's the front, I don't know—of the centipede lays discarded on the floor. The half with either longer legs or antennae pokes from his mouth.

"That's active murder face," Jonah says.

"Accurate. But, unless you're a centipede, he's too lazy to commit actual murder."

Beef leaves the room, seeming to sense that he's being gently ridiculed, and I find a set of sheets, a couple quilts and a brand new pillow still in the plastic for Jonah. He doesn't make up the couch yet because it's too early, and he sets up his video streaming account on the TV on the wall. I pick up Evie's journal and open it on my lap, reading through old entries to see if she left me any other details about the path we have to find.

THIRTY-TWO

THE CLANG OF THE LITTLE METAL THING INSIDE MY CAN of spray paint keeps me grounded in reality. Every time I shake the can, the clang follows. It feels like a drumline before a battle, and each time the percussion sounds I become more amped about the fight.

The similarities between some highly anticipated sports event and what Jonah and I face end as soon as I begin drawing them, because usually with sports you know what game you've come to play.

We do not.

We don't even know where the event will take place. Not really.

I probably should not make sports metaphors this early in the morning.

Our boots crunch on the ground, and the noise overwhelms my senses as I try too hard to listen to the barely audible sounds of nature. Walking with more intentional steps only makes the snapping of twigs and grinding of stones worse. With every step, I grow more impatient until I start feeling snappish. One wrong move, and I could lash out.

Fuck, I am so tired.

So deeply exhausted down to my marrow.

I could have easily misremembered any of the tiny little details, and the thought forces me to a halt.

"Why'd you stop? Do you see something?" Jonah asks.

When I don't respond, he comes around to face me and his eyes search mine for an answer to his questions. The leaves on the ground rise up with a gust of wind. Branches rustle, awakened.

I reach out and touch his arm to confirm he's really here.

"I ... I don't know." A truly spectacular answer.

"Is something wrong?"

"Obviously something is wrong, but I don't know where to begin explaining what. It's probably easier to say what's right at this point and let you fill in the blanks from there."

I pull my hand back and weave my fingers into tangles in my hair. I want to tear it from my head. The woods breathe again, and I search for the familiar voice blended in with the other sounds out here. Jonah's mouth doesn't move, and he doesn't say anything—neither to question me or haunt me.

"We should keep going." I try stomping down the frustration brewing inside of me. It won't get me answers any quicker if I get pissed off, though I feel about ready to explode. "We just passed the plastic bag tied around the tree, and the car isn't far beyond that."

None of the features of the forest stand out today now that I've stopped looking for anything beyond the orange marks and waypoints stuck in my head. How could anyone find their way through here without leaving markings behind to remind them of the way they've come? The deeper we go, the thicker the trees grow in together and the dirt paths get tighter until the brush whispers against our sides.

The forest—or, rather, the being within the forest—doesn't call for me like it did before. It leaves me to look at the trees for signs where I indicated finding something. The orange spots show my trail, but I left an X on the tree near the car.

"I painted this." I run my fingers across the symbol on the bark. "But there was a car here, like in Evie's journal."

Jonah steps over the tangled shrubs and goes deeper off the trail in search of the car. I don't tell him it was right here, mere inches from the tree. I don't want to admit that all I've been able to find is the plastic bag tied around the tree, and that I have to try again.

He keeps walking away, looking around until he fades nearly out of view. The trees swallow his figure and I fight the urge to panic and rush after him. He'll come back.

He'll come back.

I go over the mental list of waypoints Evie mentioned: an abandoned truck, a tree with a split trunk shaped like the letter U, a circle of spruce trees.

"We have to backtrack, I think," I say when Jonah emerges from the woods covered in burrs. "This isn't it."

We do, and this time I pay more attention to the woods around me. I use a new symbol on the trees once we split off in a new direction from the plastic bag. I make triangles as we progress down another thin trail made by wild animals.

My legs ache from the steady pace through the forest, but I force myself forward. The pain gives me something to focus on, and it keeps my mind away from thoughts of illusions and things that aren't really there. Every time I venture down that path, I risk getting stuck in the place where all of this is made up in some fucked up attempt at processing my grief.

"Wait a second," Jonah says. "I have this app on my phone that will track our path. It's designed for runners, which I tried to be for like a week before realizing that running sucks. We could use it to build a map of where we've been, in addition to your paint. You know, in case he tries to mess with the markers."

"How do we know Benjamin can't fuck up the app?" I ask.

"We go into town and look at it. I don't think he can actually change what the phone records, just what we see. That's how he messed with your pictures of the living room. If you saw mud, and it was a complete enough illusion, you believed you saw it in the pictures. I bet if we looked at the pictures we tried taking of the horse, they'd look different outside of his reach."

"That ... that actually makes a lot of sense."

Jonah begins tracking our movements on the app, and I let myself believe Benjamin doesn't have power over technology. Especially technology that didn't exist until years after he died.

The idea of having something more reliable than my own memory taking a record of our path makes me walk faster, like now I don't have to carry the weight of worrying about forgetting where I've been. Instead I wonder what the pictures of the horse would show. Do I want to know?

I decide I don't want to think about it and begin counting each tree I mark. The monotony of the process sucks me in until my only thoughts become 'spray, count, walk.'

Jonah snaps me out of my routine as I pass my twenty seventh tree.

"There it is," he says.

He points ahead to where a pile of reddish metal interrupts the otherwise pristine spread of nature. The truck. Well, it used to be a truck. Now it's only a pile of rusted metal in the vague shape of a pick up truck. When I found the car, it was the rounded type of classic car from the sixties or seventies, but this truck has the more modern look of something from maybe the eighties.

"Can you walk in a couple circles around it?" I ask Jonah.

"Why?"

"So when we look at your app, we see an obnoxious circle where this spot is on the map."

He nods and gets to walking at a brisk pace around the truck. I stand behind with my hands on my hips, taking in the sight of the truck and the surrounding paths. From our current spot, we have two options. One looks like it might loop back the way we came, so I decide we'll take the other that weaves through a patch of burned trees and short new growth. Lightning must have struck here sometime after Evie came through here, but still a while back.

"Marisa? You ready to go?"

I turn to where Jonah should be, but I find no one. He still works on his circle on the map, blissfully unaware that someone used his voice to speak to me.

He looks up, confusion on his face, without me having to say anything.

"What?" he says.

"It's happening again. The voice —*your* voice.."

We found the truck. We're on the right track. Benjamin must know that if he's decided to play with us now. Maybe he's scared.

Jonah returns to my side. "I heard you say something too."

"No, you didn't. Trust me. It's one of his tricks, like he did to me when I came out alone."

He doesn't bother going pale or looking surprised, and I guess that's it. That's where we are now with this.

"He wants us to turn around, so I say we keep going." I fake confidence when I speak, but it only barely covers the uncertainty in my voice.

"We've been out here for hours." He sits on a fallen log by the truck. "We have to go home. This will be here tomorrow."

I don't want to turn back. I want answers, and I don't want to have to wait another day for them. But, when I look up past the jagged tops of the trees, I realize I have to. Jonah's right about the sunset. It's already gotten darker without me noticing, and the light on our phones will only last so long before losing power, especially with Jonah using his GPS.

"Okay, fine."

Jonah stands and brushes dirt from the stump off his butt. He catches me looking, and there's no way for me to tell him I was zoning out for a minute without sounding like I'm trying to roll back the fact that I was kind of ogling him. I didn't mean to. The motion drew my eyes to it. Fuck, I think my mouth was open a little.

He raises both eyebrows. I die. I wish I could shrink to the size of the pretty little dried up mushrooms growing on the fallen trees nearby.

"Let's go. I don't want to be out here in the dark," is what I say instead of getting defensive or drawing any sort of attention to the last ten seconds of our lives.

"Lead the way." He holds out a hand to gesture me past him, and the stupid part of my brain decides to be convinced he does it because he doesn't want me looking at his ass the whole walk back to the house.

Shut up, stupid part of my brain. Shut up. It is perfectly reasonable for him to want me to lead the way back since I brought us all the way out here.

I rule the whole thing out as nothing more than being human. People check people out all the time without having particularly sexy feelings about them. It's perfectly normal. My subconscious was not trying to tell me something.

We walk at a brisk pace and stay silent. Even if I had the lung capacity to carry on a conversation at a speed closer to a jog than a walk, I need to put all my focus into following only the trees with orange markings. All thoughts of butts and embarrassment fade behind the immediate need to not get lost out here.

THIRTY-THREE

Jonah makes me go to the Wobbly Leg when we get back from our day in the woods, though I want to collapse on the couch with a bowl of subpar popcorn and ignore the existence of my throbbing legs. So we should leave the property to check the GPS tracker to see if our route looks different in each place, fine. Jonah makes a good point as to why we need to leave the place we know Benjamin has a hold over us, and I know it can't wait until the morning if I want to get back out there at first light, but god do I want to lie down.

Instead, we tuck our phones into our pockets and I grab my bag with my wallet and Evie's journal placed inside.

We take the table in the corner farthest from all the other people in the bar, then look at the red line on Jonah's phone that indicates the path we traveled. It looks the same as it did when we looked at the house, like Benjamin hadn't even bothered to mess it up since he knew we were onto him. Or, maybe he figured out how to reach us out here.

No, Evie said in her journal he has a certain reach. He can't touch us out here.

"I'm so tired of this," I say after our server brings us our meals. "I hate not knowing what's real and what's not."

Jonah contemplates his response through a mouthful of shepherd's pie. "We figured something out today, though. Part of how he works."

I nod, then take a bite of the cole slaw in a little bowl on the side of my plate of fried shrimp.

"What the fuck?" I spit the cole slaw into my napkin as delicately as one can possibly spit out food. "Is there pineapple in this cole slaw?"

It distracts me for a moment, fishing around in my bowl of cabbage and mayonnaise to determine if I actually tasted pineapple or if my sense of taste has gone off the deep end. It doesn't take long to find the chunk of yellow fruit mixed in with the other vegetables.

"God, that's the worst thing that's happened to me since I've arrived."

"That's an opinion, all right."

"Listen, I came here knowing I was moving into a haunted house. I did not come here knowing there would be pineapple in my cole slaw."

We laugh for a second before the reality of the situation comes back into focus.

"Okay, so all the shit he can do, he can't do it here. That's great, except for the fact that we also can't defeat him out here."

We still have one more waypoint to find before we reach the circle of spruce trees, and our memories can't be relied on as soon as we set foot on Roger's property. I guess, at this point, we should call it Benjamin's property. He rules it. He's ruled it for a long time now.

"She wrote about all the properties of the things she used to curse him, right? Especially the spruce being the core of her spell or whatever. That's supposed to mean eternal life, right?" Jonah says, flipping through the book I hand to him. "She could have given us a hint at how to stay clear despite Benjamin's attempts at tricking us."

"I think Benjamin tricked her before she realized what she'd done. I think he tricked her and Roger and anyone else who spent any time in that house, and that's probably another reason why the kids don't want anything to do with the place."

Jonah shrugs. "Okay, that's probably accurate."

"But if her whole thing is based on the properties of plants, then maybe there is a plant we can use for, I don't know, clarity." All I know about curses and witchcraft comes from a limited array of media, any or all of which could be completely fictional. I feign confidence yet again for the sake of making some kind of progress. Even if what I know came from fiction, doesn't it all have roots in the truth?

I take the journal back and look through the entries, more out of habit than anything. Evie didn't know how to stop him. Beyond taking his bones so he couldn't undo his curse, I doubt she knew the severity of what she did. This whole town thinks she was a monster, and, for a while, I thought she was simply misunderstood. Now, I know she was just as bad as Benjamin. Maybe worse, if for nothing other than having created him.

There can be nothing left of him.

A line in an entry near the end catches my attention.

"What do you think this means?" I point at the words and ask Jonah.

"I think we probably have to get rid of the remains."

"Right, but how do we get rid of bones?"

"I don't know."

Silence fills the space between us as our server returns to ask if we want another beer, which we most definitely want but don't need.

"We need to make a plan," Jonah says.

"Okay. Like what? Figure out if there's something that will keep Benjamin out of our heads?"

"As a starting point. Then we go out and see what's left of him. Maybe there's more than bones to dispose of."

I turn my attention back to my meal and try forcing myself to eat more. The shrimp is too greasy and over fried, the fries were never quite warmed and definitely came from a bag, and the cole slaw still has pineapple in it. Too bad Benjamin hadn't made me hallucinate the pineapple and what I have here is a perfectly acceptable cole slaw.

The only salvageable thing on my plate is the pickle, which I eat slowly while scrolling through my phone.

Our server brings our beers, and I take a sip before realizing I don't want it anymore.

I open my photos app and scroll through what I've taken since getting here. The majority of the shots contain Beef sleeping in a variety of positions.

The horse.

Oh my god.

"Jonah. Look at the pictures of the horse."

If I had been eating, I'd have choked. I still might.

"What?" he asks.

"Chew and swallow your food, then look at the pictures of the horse."

My voice comes out too calm and too soft, despite the fact that I should be freaking out.

"What are you talking about?" He unlocks his phone and starts scrolling.

We knew there was something wrong with the pictures we took. We both saw the blur. We know he can only mess with what we see, but not with what technology captures.

I don't know what I expected when I looked back at them here, but it wasn't this.

"There is no horse."

THIRTY-FOUR

JONAH GETS TO EXPERIENCE THE GUTTURAL SCREAMS OF Beef as I pack him into his carrier and leave the cabin. He repacks his overnight bag and tosses it in the backseat. Most of the things I pack into the back of Jonah's car belong to the cat except for my two plants and clothes, just like when I came here in the first place. Carefully, I pocket the bones I found and pray to whomever's in charge that we don't get pulled over, because I can't explain having some dude's finger bones in the pocket of my jeans.

I take one last look at the horse before I head back up to the driveway where the Subaru idles. Hellie and Jack saw the horse. Jonah saw it. Yet it still doesn't really exist.

Seeing the animal out there, standing with her head over the half-door to her stall, twists my stomach. Despite knowing what she is—rather, what she *isn't*—leaving still feels wrong. It feels like abandonment. Like neglect.

"I can't do this," I say. "I can't leave her here alone. What if she's real?"

Jonah faces me with his hands on my shoulders to steady me. "She's not. You know she's not."

"She ate all the food we brought. She drank her water." I've seen the mice in the barn, the spills on the floor from the horse splashing her nose in the bucket. The absence of the nourishment I left for her comes with an explanation, but I hate it.

"We have to go. It's not safe here."

"How could I fall for this? How did we all fall for it?" I ask. I need an answer.

"I don't know."

If Benjamin, somehow, is still alive, I'd like to kick his ass.

JONAH LIVES IN A STUDIO APARTMENT ABOVE A laundromat I didn't know the town even had, and it smells like dryer sheets and 6-in-1 man shampoo. His work vest hangs on a coat rack by the doorway of the large room, along with a matching green visor I've never seen him wear. It has a gaudy button on it that says, "I'm a Garden Expert" and I kind of want to make fun of him for it.

"I'm sorry there's not much space in here," he says. "You can set Beef up wherever."

He takes the litter box and sets it down near the bathroom. I let Beef out of his carrier. The cat wanders slowly around the apartment in search of his food bowls, which I stuffed in my suitcase with the half empty bag of food, and he yowls again when he can't find them. It doesn't take long for him to return to my side and stare up at me with a silent demand.

Once the cat has food and water and my plants have a sunny spot in the window, I lean my suitcase by the door and make for the one armchair in the apartment carrying Evie's journal. Now, in this safe place, I have to read it again and make sure I didn't misread anything.

Her entries remain the same, and I breathe a sigh of relief that everything I learned from her remains stagnant. At least something hasn't changed.

"Why wouldn't he have changed what I read here?" I ask.

Jonah joins me, taking a seat on one upholstered arm of the chair. "Huh?"

"The journal. He didn't mess with it. The entries are the same as the ones I read at the cabin."

I show him and, in response, he lifts the journal to his nose and takes a deep inhale.

"What the hell are you doing?" I ask.

"If Benjamin didn't change it, maybe he couldn't."

"And smelling a dead lady's journal will tell you … what?"

"The paper could be made with herbs, or maybe an essential oil was drizzled on it. Something to protect it."

Before Jonah continues smelling Evie's journal, I take it back and flip through the last entries. Her writing ends before the halfway point in the pages, and it turns to madness before it stops all together.

I made a monster. I am a monster.
Roger isn't safe. No one is safe from me.

The last entries read like decay. The words fall apart with

letters missing or in the wrong place. Sentences have gaps in them where she skipped something. The ink has been stabbed into the pages with the violence of an angry, dying woman.

There can be nothing left of him.
There can be nothing left of me.

Incoherent half-thoughts run up the sides of the pages. They curl into themselves, ignoring the faded lines on the paper. Evie writes as the words come to her, disjointed and manic and chaotic.

Burn me.

The last complete thoughts Evie wrote repeats like a mantra for two full pages before the pen starts running out of ink and fading.

"If she knew how to protect the journal, wouldn't she have protected herself too?" I say.

Jonah looks at the book and inspects the tea stain on the pages. "Unless whatever protected the book was accidental. A spill, maybe. I can't tell what made this mark, but my guess is some kind of tea."

I open a text to Elise anyway, but I haven't spoken to her in so long so I close the message as soon as I'd opened it. What normal person knows the kind of tea their great uncle and great aunt prefer? Especially since Evie disappeared before Elise was born.

Burn me. Burn me. Burnmeburnme.

"What if we're supposed to burn the journal?" Jonah suggests. "That would make sense, I think. It's like a token of what she did, and maybe burning it cuts the ties between Evie or Benjamin and this place."

"Or, what if everything in here is a lie?" I say. "What if Evie's side of the story is only what she wants whoever reads this to think happened? She could be leading us astray with this."

Jonah frowns, because, at this point, my thought has merit. We've found nothing to prove anything Evie has written, except for the bones. We don't really know if we can trust this long vanished version of her. I don't want to trust her.

"What if we can't trust anything this book says?" I ask.

"We don't have anything else to go off. We have to hope this is the truth."

I close the book, then lean my head back against the chair and shut my eyes. Behind my eyelids, the words BURN ME fill the darkness in Evie's manic handwriting.

The words show no signs of fading, though I want to sleep. Try to, at least. I remind myself that I should be safe here. Benjamin cannot force upon me more nightmares of being buried, of choking. He can't reach me.

"So, only one problem with my place," Jonah says, apparently realizing a flaw in tonight's plan. "I don't have a couch."

His words wake me from the near sleep I'd drifted into.

"Okay?" I say before it dawns on me.

The entire apartment is this one room, aside from the bathroom, and the only furniture consists of the chair we'd been sitting in and the queen sized bed where Beef currently sleeps in the center.

"Oh." I realize. "Um, well. We're adults. No reason for one of us to get a shit night of sleep on the floor, when we're *adults*."

Am I an adult? Is that what I am? The word feels so loaded in this context, and I don't like it.

"As long as you're okay with it, I am," Jonah says.

"Yeah. Yeah sure. We have Purity Beef anyway. We just have to leave room."

"For Purity Beef."

"Yes. For Purity Beef."

The cat looks up at us and narrows his eyes, displeased at being ridiculed in such a way that likens him to a tool of religious chastity. Evidently, the cat is very progressive.

"You're lucky Jonah let you come," I say to the cat. "So don't look at me like that."

Really, this shouldn't be as daunting as it is. Sharing a bed with a friend shouldn't concern me after everything I've seen since moving here. Illusions and hallucinations and ghosts should be more alarming than this. There isn't anything to be afraid of here, it's only a comfortable place to sleep for me and the guy who's helping me un-haunt my own place. Nothing sexy. Just sleep.

THIRTY-FIVE

WHEN I WAKE, I NOTICE TWO THINGS: THE RUMBLING warmth of Beef half sprawled over my stomach, and the cool dampness of drool on cloth. I lift a hand to my face to wipe the saliva off my cheek, and find the pillow my face has soaked isn't actually a pillow.

My eyes snap open in horror.

I left room for the cat, but still managed to fall asleep on Jonah.

I drooled on his shoulder.

Oh my god.

"Are you awake?" a groggy voice asks.

"No." Fuck. "Yes, obviously. I'm sorry. Oh my god, I'm disgusting." I push myself up and away and, for some reason, try and dab at the damp spot on his t-shirt with my t-shirt.

He laughs. At me, not with me, because I'm not laughing. I am slowly dying of embarrassment. All the actual horror movie shit I've been living doesn't come close to stacking up to this moment on the list of The Worst Things I've Ever Experienced.

"You clearly needed the rest," he says with a voice still coarse from having been asleep mere seconds ago himself.

I rub my eyes and try combing my bedhead down with my fingers, but the damage has already been done.

"Why didn't you make me move?"

"Well, there was a girl sized dead weight passed out on my shoulder, and I was scrolling through obituaries for a bit before I also fell asleep."

"You were what?"

"Well, I thought maybe reading about how Roger died might shed some light on all of this."

"I thought he died of natural causes. I didn't get the sense from Elise that anything, you know, unusual happened."

"He died of a heart attack, or at least that's what the obituary says."

My mind lingers on that fact for a minute before it fires off the classic Windows XP startup sound and produces an idea. It hits me hard.

"Lemongrass."

Jonah blinks. "Lemongrass?"

"My dad drank lemongrass tea for his cholesterol, because the doctor said it might help. He had heart disease. It's what killed him. The heart disease, not the lemongrass tea."

"I'm sorry."

"No. I mean, thank you. But no, I mean, what if the tea spilled on the journal was lemongrass? Could it have some spiritual property or something?"

It's too early for complete optimism, but, at this point,

I'll try anything if it means finding the end of this nightmare.

"Oh, shit. Maybe."

Having found something to distract me from the drool left on Jonah's shoulder, we both retrieve our phones and start scouring all the websites about the properties of lemongrass.

It doesn't take long for one of us to find something useful. While the plant's medicinal qualities don't help us now, Jonah finds a website where it's said to boost clarity. The two of us go down a wikipedia rabbit hole until eventually we find a corner of the internet where neither of us truly belong. It contains recipes for a tea for clarity, including lemongrass and dried cinnamon.

We sit there for a little bit, Beef still purring away in the space between our criss-crossed legs, and digest the information. Lemongrass and cinnamon tea sounds reasonable. It might taste good. Hell, it might even make me feel better for once.

"Listen, I'm going to run to the store and see if they have the tea. I think I have cinnamon in the drawer, but actually that might be expired so I'll get that too. Uh, you should stay here. I won't be gone long."

Though I don't love the idea of being alone, I also relish it. A warm shower without the presence of Benjamin lurking right outside sounds like a dream.

Jonah shows me where the extra towels are and tells me how to get the water to a temperature somewhere between scalding and icy, then leaves on his quest for tea. I didn't want to tell him my doubts about the little grocery store in town having a wide assortment of teas beyond Irish Breakfast and Sleepy Time, because I didn't want to dash his hopes. Maybe he'll surprise me.

I follow Jonah's instructions to start the shower and let

the steam fill the room around me while I scrub my face and brush my teeth. Even though the water feels like it could burn off a layer of my skin in the process of getting me clean, I savor it.

Once I dry myself off and dress myself in clean jeans and an oversized t-shirt, I feel okay. I feel like I can finish something.

Before I realize what I've done, I hit the green call button on the screen of my phone with Brent's number typed in. I can't fix my situation with the monster right now, but I can tell Brent off once and for all instead of letting him think there's still some chance I might cave and hand him the money he wants.

I sit on the edge of the tub and eagerly wait for him to answer.

"Uh, yeah?" he answers, sleepy. How considerate of me to forget about the time difference when it's already absurdly early.

"I hung up on you last time you called, so I wanted to make it clear to you that I will not be sending you any money to fix your water heater. I want you to delete my number and forget about me, because I'm done. Really done. Your house is your problem, and you made it that way when you left my name off all the documents." I sound far more confident than I am, considering my lack of sleep and lack of preparation for the conversation.

"Hold on," he says. I hear a shuffling on the other end, like he's getting out of bed. Another voice asks where he's going. "What are you talking about?"

"You called me twice asking for money to fix your water heater so you could sell the place. Are you seriously playing dumb with me right now?"

"I never called you, except for one butt dial. The house is already under contract to sell."

My bones quake with frustration, but I keep my voice steady.

"Oh fuck off with that. I can tell you the exact times and dates of the calls. Durations if you'd like."

I flip the call to speaker and go into my call history. Though I deleted his voicemails, I didn't clear out the calls. At least, I didn't think so. They aren't listed anymore. His number appears once in the call log, and I think back to where I was at the time of the call. When Jonah and I went to get lobster, Brent called me then and hung up before it could get to voicemail.

What does it mean if he's telling the truth about not calling me?

"Actually, you know what. I don't owe you an explanation or whatever. Just … whatever. Okay? Don't contact me again. Don't try and find me. I don't owe you anything."

"That won't be hard, considering I didn't call you." The way he speaks, slow and measured, tells me he's trying not to raise his voice. "Matter of fact, we were doing good not bothering one another until just now when you decided you needed to start trouble at five am. I take it you haven't found someone to cater to your desperate need for attention, then?"

"Fuck off."

"Either that, or you've leveled up your crazy and imagined entire phone conversations so you could make me into the bad guy. I know that's another favorite hobby of yours."

"I'm not crazy. I never was crazy." I mean to convince myself, not him.

This was a bad idea. This was a horrible idea.

But I'm in it now.

"Keep telling yourself that if it makes you feel better, but you need therapy or to be locked away in a rubber room somewhere you can't suck everyone into your shit like quicksand. You're sad? That's not everyone else's problem. Unhappy with your crappy little life? Figure it out, Marisa. You think I'm the only one to blame here? I know I fucked up, but look at yourself. You'd roll over and die if it meant you didn't have to fight anymore. You're the queen of taking the easy route and letting other people make choices for you so you can blame them when you're miserable."

I have no words in my throat, no air in my lungs. Of all the things I want to say, to blame him for, I chose silence. There is no reasoning with him, especially when he might be a little bit right.

"Well, good talk. Now if you'll excuse me, I'm going back to sleep."

When the call ends, I throw the phone across the room, not hard enough to break it—because the part of me that has no money still overrides the absolute furnace of rage building up inside me—but enough that it lands on the ground with a thud. Then, I let out an earth shattering scream of frustration into a balled up towel.

CHAPTER

THIRTY-SIX

THANKS TO THE DUMB ASS MOMENT OF CONFIDENCE THAT made me call Brent, I don't know how much time passes. Jonah doesn't come back, though I wait for him, and it could be a normal period of time or it could be days. Instead of looking at the clock on my phone, which still sits against the wall where it fell, I curl up on the floor of the bathroom and lock the door.

Brent never called.

All the calls were Benjamin tormenting me, and I should have seen it sooner.

He thrives on deceit and torment. On bending the truth just enough to stay believable. He only knew my version of Brent, the version I was angry with. Benjamin didn't know that there was a Brent I once loved, and that wasn't the same person I left in Wisconsin. The monster used my anger as a weapon and turned it back on me.

Beef meows at me from outside the bathroom, and I

212

hear the faint sound of the door to the apartment unlocking, then opening, then closing. Footsteps come into the space and remind me of the day in the tub when I felt piles of dirt being dropped on my body until I could do nothing but breathe them in.

Terror seizes me as all rational thought disappears.

"Marisa? Are you okay in there?"

I ignore the voice. It's the same as the one in the forest. The one that taunted me. The one that tried to drive a stake between me and the only person out here I trust.

Next comes a knock on the door, then pounding.

Then the lock pops and a presence enters and lays eyes on me.

I feel them.

I scream.

Something strong lifts me to my feet, and I am moved — maybe by my own two legs, maybe by something else.

"Marisa. It's me."

The voice speaks to me from underwater. Or above. I don't know.

"It's okay."

Panic seizes my entire chest, my lungs and my heart and all the connected parts. It turns to hands on my throat, tighter and tighter until I can't breathe.

My vision goes dark around the edges, and my head swims.

I can't breathe.

"What happened?"

I can't.

"Marisa?"

Breathe.

Some kind of signal reaches my hand and I clasp whatever is nearest. Fabric. Warm. Soft.

I can't breathe.

Gentle hands bring my head to rest somewhere soft, and the rest of my body relaxes. The jabbing pain in my heart fades, not immediately, but eventually, and I find the strength to open my eyes.

Somehow, I've moved from the bathroom floor to Jonah's bed, leaned against the headboard with my hands in my lap. He sits upright beside me.

Everything hurts. My throat feels raw all the way down to the bottom of my esophagus. Stomach acid burns its way up and eats at my insides.

"What happened?" I ask, barely.

"I came back and you were on the floor in the bathroom. I think you had a panic attack."

"I locked the door." It sounds like an accusation, though I mean it more as a recited fact.

"I'm sorry. You didn't answer and I thought … I don't know what I thought, but I was worried."

He chokes up, and maybe on another day I might have grilled him for it as a joke. Today, weak like death and exhausted, I let it slide.

"I talked to Brent." I push myself up so I sit beside him, leaning against the headboard. "It was bad."

"He called?" Jonah doesn't skip a beat.

"Um. No. Not exactly."

I tell him about the calls I'd hallucinated where Brent asked for money and I was ready to figure out a way to help because it would be easier to get rid of him if he didn't need anything from me. Embarrassment creeps in when I tell him about how I called today to tell Brent off once and for all and, instead, got told off myself.

A violent, ice-water chill of anxiety fills my body and sloshes in my stomach. It grips me so tight and freezes me in place.

"He said I don't bother fighting shit so I can blame other people when things go wrong."

"Oh. What a dick."

"He is a dick. But he's right." My eyes sting. "I wish I could move on and not deal with this anymore, but I can't …" Every named emotions hits me in the chest at once, and I lose my last thread of composure. "I don't know anymore. Benjamin or whatever made me imagine Brent calling me about money, and he made me think you were bad too. I thought you were another illusion when you came home. I thought you were going to hurt me, even though I should've known this place is safe. Am I that easy to trick?"

My face goes hot in contrast with the rest of me, and tears stream down as if a dam has broken beneath their pressure. Everything has been too much for a long time, and I can't carry it anymore. I can't unhear the disgust in Brent's voice from when we talked earlier. Can't forget the muffled question of the new girl in his bed. Moving on seems to be so easy for him. Why can't it be easy for me too?

I vaguely notice Jonah shift beside me. My shoulder registers the warmth of a hand. "Do you … can I hug you?"

As soon as he asks, I let myself fall into him. His arms fold around me and he leans his cheek against the top of my head.

"Why are you doing this?" I ask. "Helping me?"

"It's the right thing to do."

"No. I mean, maybe. But you hardly know me, and all you want is to make this town better, but instead you're ghost hunting with me. You don't want to do this."

He nods. "I know. I don't. I never wanted to get involved in this, but I just …" He trails off. "I'm sick of bad things happening here. First Bri, and now this. Evie and

Benjamin and whoever the fuck else is out there have taken enough."

I think this is the first time I've heard Jonah use the 'fuck' word, and it startles me into silence.

"I told you about Bri. Hellie and Jack's daughter who died. It wasn't fair. She went snowshoeing in the woods behind her house like she usually did in the winter. When she went alone, she took Peony with her because the dog looks like a beast. She was smart. Anyway, there was a guy on a snowmobile out there, drunk off his ass, and he hit her."

My stomach drops through the floor. "He hit her? With a snowmobile?"

Jonah nods, face pale and eyes glassy and unfocused. "The guy, he called his buddies and just left her out there pinned beneath his crumpled sled like she was nothing. I guess she died instantly, but I don't know if that's just something they tell people because it's easier than being told they suffered."

He clenches his fists, and I want to take his hand and tell him it wasn't his fault. He couldn't have prevented it. He couldn't have known. Instead, my vocal cords are frozen in my throat and I can't even apologize.

The last puzzle piece explaining his passion for the community suddenly clicks into place. His friend went out alone, and she didn't come back. He wants to make it so that never happens again.

"We only knew because Peony came home alone and was losing her absolute shit when Jack tried bringing her in."

"I'm so sorry, Jonah. That's horrible. It's not your fault though, you know that right?"

"I know. I know it's not."

This time, I do take his hand in what I hope is a

comforting gesture. His hand is coarse from work, but still soft somehow. All this time, I had no idea. Knowing wouldn't have made anything different, we'd still be here trying to end a curse so we could live our lives in peace.

We stay like that a while, wordlessly. Two broken people separated only by a purring cinderblock of a cat.

THIRTY-SEVEN

AFTER FAILING AT THE GROCERY STORE AS EXPECTED, Jonah was lucky enough to get a box of lemongrass tea from Tanner at the diner, where it had been stashed away at the back of the shelf designated for employee snacks. The best by date came and went long before we knew we needed it, but it beats not having it at all.

Lemongrass tea tastes entirely like grass and not nearly enough like lemon. Add in the cinnamon, and by the second cup I consider the idea that dying in whatever way Benjamin has planned may be preferable to drinking stale grassy dirt juice. I don't say that aloud. Nor do I suggest we add whiskey for a lemongrass tea hot toddy. Partaking in hard liquor seems inappropriate considering today we've decided to take a recovery day before going back out in the woods.

Instead, we add honey in hopes of making it taste a bit

less like shit, then each drink another cup hoping it might help keep our heads clear.

Evie's actions seem to fixate around plants and nature, so I assume that's the type of magic she used. She can only tell us what she left in her journal, and we can only hope we interpreted it correctly.

Or maybe, I've got this all wrong and she didn't use magic at all. The idea that she chose her words to mislead us lingers in the back of my mind.

We won't know if the tea will keep us free of Benjamin's influence until we go out there.

WHEN WE GO BACK TO ROGER'S HOUSE, JONAH FILLS A backpack with bottled water and energy bars, both of which he extracts from a plastic bag from his trip to the grocery store with THANK YOU printed multiple times on its front. So much for going solely to pick up tea.

"How long do you think we're going to be out there for?" I ask after I count four big bottles and twelve bars.

"Better to be over prepared."

I don't know what he thinks will happen when we go back into the woods, but I let it go. At least he's coming with me. The look in his eyes when I asked if he was ready contradicted the "sure" that came out of his mouth.

While Jonah finishes stuffing his bag, I add to my own. I tuck Evie's journal in one of the front pockets. Along with the journal, I take one of the water bottles. Then I rummage through the kitchen for something to defend myself with. Even though I still have the five iron, I find a pink chef's knife with a plastic blade guard and take that instead.

I leave the finger bones at Jonah's apartment intentionally. Today is for discovery.

"You good?" Jonah asks as I pull my arm through the sleeve of my coat and zip it to my chin.

"Not really. Let's roll."

It goes against all my instincts to walk past the barn without checking for the horse. Even if she isn't real, I feel responsible still.

The barn feels off as we head toward the trees, but I don't let myself look. The fact that the building housed what I thought was an animal sent to, I don't know, make me reconnect with my past passion only makes this worse.

Without Beef here, without my plants, without the horse, it feels like a totally different place. Like a place I've only been in half-remembered dreams.

Our boots crunch sticks scattered along the forest floor. Each sharp crack breaks the silence for a moment and gives away our presence, not that we have any delusions of finding this altar without being noticed.

As we walk, I alternate between looking at the ground so I don't fall and checking out my surroundings for anything interesting. For a while, I don't see anything but the usual, and it makes me think about the piles of earth in the house, the mouthfuls of damp soil. How? No matter how many ways I tell myself it didn't really happen, I can't let the memory go.

"I hate coming out here," I say.

We reach the truck without incident, though things I know aren't there skitter at the edges of my vision. Shadows of creatures run past in dark blurs. New, translucent visions try overlapping with reality. Benjamin's illusions remain, but not as strong as before.

The lemongrass seems to be working a bit. It takes the

edge off Benjamin's torment. It draws a line between real and not.

"It's got a dark atmosphere. Heavy and ominous, like something bad definitely happened out here," I continue.

"Yeah. It does not have good vibes."

"Vibes? Seriously? Are you applying Life Is Good™ logic to my situation right now? Will you make me a knockoff t-shirt with a disapproving golden retriever that says some shit like 'wow. Bad vibes'?"

"It would have to be a dad hat. Nantucket red."

I chuckle a little. "What the hell is Nantucket red? Actually, first off, what is Nantucket?"

"Nantucket is an island off the coast of Massachusetts. Very bougie. And Nantucket red is this distressed pinkish reddish color that only places that also sell ironic and punny lobster t-shirts are allowed to have in stock."

"Sounds like … you know what, no. I don't even know what to make of this." I'm holding back laughter now, and, as usual, I don't know if he's telling the truth or making shit up for the fun of it.

"It's a very classy color. You put on a pair of Nantucket red shorts from Vineyard Vines and some boat shoes and everyone knows you come from a yacht family. Or at least a family with a membership to a nice golf club."

"I see you've put a lot of thought into the cultural implications of a shade of red named after an island."

"If you had something like, I don't know, Mall Of America blue, you'd have opinions about it. Like there'd be certain people you associate with your Mall Of America blue and it would evoke a physical reaction from you."

"Oh my god, fuck off. Is that the only tourist attraction you can think of from the Midwest?"

"Yes, because it is."

I smack his arm a little and he pretends to be wounded.

It almost feels like we're not wandering the woods looking for a cursed altar so we could figure out how to stop a man's ghost from terrorizing me.

"One day, I'll drag you out there and show you all the cool stuff we have." I make a list in my head. Mount Rushmore obviously sucks. If you count Wyoming as the Midwest, there's Yellowstone and the Tetons. The Badlands are solid. All National parks though. Surely we have other things to do. Museums or something. I hardly remember any of this. How much of my life before this did I bury in the parts of my memory that I can't reach?

"I'll hold you to it."

We fall back into silence as we redirect our focus to following the trail. At this point, the dirt is no longer visible as we wander through a divide in the brush.

The lightness of the moment fades, replaced by a heavy sense of dread. Something bad lurks just around one of the trees up ahead. I know it in the pit of my stomach.

I stop walking, feigning thirst, and take a long drink from the water bottle I stuck in my bag. Whatever lies ahead, I don't want to face it, but I can't waste more time without Jonah noticing.

"I have a bad feeling," I say.

"Me too."

I swallow the fear and press forward. I tell myself Benjamin isn't stupid. He knows we're coming for him, and he wants us to turn back. This means we're going the right way.

We find the U-shaped tree with the split trunk next, and Jonah walks a few circles around it in case we need the app to remind us of its location later.

The air thickens as trees grow in tighter, a crowd closing in on us until we suffocate. I shut my eyes tight, clench my fists against a wave of claustrophobia. These branches could smother me the way the soil did that night in the tub.

"I think we're almost there," I say. "I really feel it now."

What I feel, I can't articulate. Is the weight on my skin Benjamin? It is Evie? Is it nothing more than my imagination filling in gaps in the story.

It only takes another quarter mile before we reach a bunch of spruce trees. They thicken as we progress forward, then, as suddenly as they came on, they stop. The path deposits us in the center of a clearing surrounded by a ring of evergreens.

Before us stands a tall stone smoothed from decades of weather. Once brightly colored rope has been wrapped around the stone four times and tied in a knot. A body—or, what once was a body and now is only a pile of bones and the tattered remains of a pair of rubber boots and other unidentified clothing—lays prone on the ground within a circle of charred ground.

"Oh my god. That's a skeleton." I should be more surprised. A normal person would still be surprised to find the remains of someone out in the woods, even if that's what they expected to find.

Jonah freezes at the slight opening in the trees where the path cut through.

"This isn't Benjamin though," I say. "I'm no expert on 90s fashion, but this looks like a woman's jacket."

Though I gesture with my hand to the bright fabric, I don't touch it.

"And the boots." I point to the body's feet then my own. "They look a bit smaller than my size."

I venture forward, closer to the stone and inspect the area at the base of it by prodding around the ground with a long, fallen branch. More bones. Another pair of rubber soled boots that might've once had leather at the tops, but it's long been eaten away. These ones look bigger, like they'd fit a man's foot.

"Evie said she bound Benjamin to the stone while he died. So this must be him," I say.

Jonah hasn't moved from the edge of the clearing.

"That means the other body is, probably, Evie."

It should feel more climactic to have found her, to have solved the mystery of where she went, but I can't shake a different thought nagging at me.

This place had caught fire. Not the circle of trees, nor the surrounding forest. A circle, perfect as far as my eye can tell, of blackened grasses fills the clearing. Upon closer inspection, the bodies' boots have been burned, but not to the point of melting.

"She forgot the bones," Jonah says.

"Yeah. And she didn't start a hot enough fire to disintegrate the remains."

THIRTY-EIGHT

EVEN THOUGH WE'LL HAVE ACCESS TO THE INTERNET IN A matter of hours, I fixate on how to make a fire hot enough to turn bones to ashes. The crunchy autumn leaves atop the charred ground might help, as will the fact that the bones have had almost two decades to dry up in the sun. What else? How do I do this without burning the whole forest down?

Will it stay within the confines of the ring like Evie's fire did?

I watch the orange markings on the trees pass as we walk, and I consider whether or not I'm willing to start a forest fire.

At this point, I think I might be.

A whisper buzzes past me, a familiar voice. Not Jonah's this time. Brent's? Not recent Brent, but the Brent from years ago. When we liked one another because things were new and we hadn't fucked them up yet. We'd listen to pop punk music and talk about which songs were 'ours.' We'd caption our social media posts with emo lyrics, and he'd sing them to me while we wasted time in one of our rooms.

"You can't do it," he says. "You're not strong enough."

No.

I come to a halt and cover my ears with my palms. Brent's voice creeps in.

It's just a voice, I tell myself. Benjamin hasn't gained the strength to make me see things. We've managed to stave off the worst of it.

Another day, maybe two, and this ends.

"What's wrong?" Jonah asks when he catches up. "Why'd you stop?"

I shake the other voice off. "Had a rock in my boot."

While we stand in the middle of nowhere, we look at Jonah's app and see we've made it halfway back to the house.

Almost done.

I resume walking at as fast a pace as my legs will allow. My lungs feel raw from the chill in the air scraping against them with each breath. Every muscle in my body burns from exertion.

"Do you think you'll stay in town when this is done?" Jonah asks.

The question is a solid distraction, because I hadn't thought about it since I got here. Beyond swearing I wouldn't take Beef on another road trip, I never considered what I'd do after I found Evie and ended the curse. Will I stay?

"I don't know." It's the truth, but when I turn I see Jonah's face has fallen a little. "I have to find a job, and a more permanent living situation. There's so much I have to do, and I don't know where to start with any of it."

Plus, I don't think I can bear living in Roger's house

after this. It'll still be haunted, passively, by ghosts who don't exist outside my memory. They'll hang around every corner, reminding me of what happened there. They'll remind me of bones and visions. Of all the bad things.

"If I don't stay, I'll keep in touch. I'll visit."

I've barely kept in touch with Elise. At this point, I wouldn't say we're still friends. Acquaintances, perhaps, but not more than that. We worked together, and built something off the forced proximity and shared corporate misery. Without that, we have no foundation.

Will it be the same with Jonah? Will we drift apart when we don't share this common goal?

Something metal catches my attention, and I tell Jonah to hang back on the trail before I veer off our barely worn path to get a better look. For all I know, it could be nothing, but after so many hours spent out here, I won't risk missing something important.

In the distance, I hear a dog barking.

It's not possible. Nobody lives out here.

I approach the glint of metal and find the source. Paint that was once a pristine red chips off the remains of a snowmobile. It lays on its side, front end crumpled against the tree that ended its journey. My stomach drops.

I know what this is.

The tea didn't work. Benjamin had been waiting for the right moment to show us our failure, and the story is still so fresh in my mind that it must have been easy for him to draw it out and make it real.

"Fuck. Oh fuck."

All my composure from earlier evaporates and I descend into panic at the sight before me. This is more than decades old bones. This is worse.

Beside the snowmobile, a girl lies facedown on the ground. One of the skis pins her to the forest floor. Her arm is bent at an unnatural angle. A pool of blood trickles from the front of her, probably from her nose.

No.

He can't do this.

"Don't come over here!" I call, too late.

Jonah has already seen what I've found.

He rushes toward the body and tries freeing the dead girl from the weight of the machine. He has to know this isn't real. He can't save her. This is all Benjamin, using Jonah's guilt to torture him too.

"Jonah. Stop! It's not her."

I try and pull him off the ground, but he thrashes out of my grip and goes back to trying to save a girl who's been dead for years.

"It's not her! It's not real," I say.

He doesn't acknowledge my words, but he stops fighting the weight of the snowmobile and falls down to his knees. His body quakes with a wail. I go to his side and take one of his hands in mine, but he doesn't notice. His grief consumes him as he stares down at the scene of his best friend's death. Nothing I say will fix this.

THIRTY-NINE

Jonah isn't okay.

When he finally tries to stand, he sways on his feet and I catch him before he loses balance. He barely holds onto me as I position his arm over my shoulders so I can keep him upright.

"I'm sorry," I say.

He doesn't say anything in response.

I guide him slowly to a fallen log and help him sit back down. He catches his head in his hands and deflates again, not that he had recovered much from the initial shock of what we saw.

"Is this what it been like for you?" Jonah asks so quietly I almost don't hear.

"He doesn't have anything as traumatic to throw at me. Just Brent. Um, and I guess dying. This is worse."

Jonah nods, then glances back at the wreckage.

"Why would someone do this?" he asks.

"Because he's a monster. He was a monster before whatever Evie did to him, and time only made him worse."

"Evie should have let him rot in prison for murder instead."

"I think she was as bad as him in the end. She couldn't have been reasoned with."

It takes all I have to be reasonable and calm. What I want to say is Benjamin deserved a thousand deaths if this is any indication of what he was like in life. What I want to say is I hope it hurts when we kill him for the last time. I don't say any of that though, because it won't help.

A light rain begins, and I pull my hood up and hug my jacket tighter to my body. I don't want to be out here anymore. I don't want to do this.

I could leave town and forget about everything. Instead of fighting, I could go.

But Jonah ... I brought him into this. I can't abandon him now.

The anger in me might be all that keeps me going now —anger that Benjamin delayed my fresh start in life, and, more so, that he was so cruel in showing Jonah the death of his friend. I doubt Benjamin has any humanity left in him now, but I want him to regret the things he's done. That's all I have left to push me forward.

"We're not dressed for the rain," I say. "Come on."

It takes a minute, but he eventually rises and we start walking again.

The dampness in the air clings to my jeans, and the chill bites the places where water has already soaked through. I hate early spring. I hate it back home and I hate it here. It's wet and cold and the combination cuts like knives.

The silence between us amplifies the dread constricting around my chest. I wish I knew what to say, or that I could at least promise we wouldn't come across anymore horrible scenes. When we come back here, we won't have the imagined protection of the lemongrass. It'll only be us and Benjamin, and he'll know why we've come.

So instead, I keep my mouth shut and occasionally turn around to be sure Jonah's still behind me on the path only wide enough for us to go single file.

By the time we return, the rain has stopped and a sharp wind has taken its place. The temperature drops to the point where the damp fabric of our clothes stiffens, and my hands begin to go numb.

Jonah doesn't say a word as I help him into the passenger's seat of the Subaru and fasten the seatbelt.

I keep telling myself I'm in control right now. This is real.

I'll get us out of here.

I don't even fuck with the driver's seat before I pull out onto the road and drive away. Jonah keeps his seat far too close to the steering wheel, but right now all I care about is how it makes it easier to slam my foot down on the accelerator.

We're getting out of here.

I forget the way to Jonah's apartment, and I miss the little side road twice and the turn for the driveway once. Even once I've parked and turned off the ignition, my heart slams in my chest like Benjamin might still catch me.

"We have to go inside. Let's go."

Jonah tries exiting the car, but forgets about his still buckled seatbelt. The two of us are disasters.

We get inside, and Jonah sits on the ground beside

Beef. The cat senses the grief in him and curls against his thigh.

My stomach growls, but I ignore it. I sit on the floor with Jonah and pick up my phone. Evie gave us a hint in her final attempt at getting rid of Benjamin. Her fire didn't burn hot enough, and in her madness she forgot the bones to complete his skeleton for the last ritual.

I'll remember them. I will be enough.

While I scroll the internet for ways to start a really hot fire, I wander Jonah's apartment in search of backpack sized items to bring on our walk tomorrow. A half empty bottle of gin fits nicely in the pack, as does a plastic container of charcoal lighter fluid.

"Amazing," I laugh to myself. "Booze, lighter fluid, a kitchen knife, and some guy's bones. This will make a good story for the cops."

I've officially gone off the rails. Fully and completely.

Not like Evie though. Never like her.

I'm cleaning up her mess, not getting revenge.

The internet tells me way more than I thought I'd want to know about burning bones. I say a silent promise to the FBI agent tasked with monitoring my search history, telling them I'm undoing an old curse and not doing actual arson. Please understand, FBI agent. You must know I'd never do something like this if I didn't have a good reason.

I find myself pacing again, like I've grown accustomed to doing over the last weeks—god, I've only been here a few weeks. It feels like months, at least. Years. I'd believe it if Jonah told me we've known one another for a decade.

He still sits slumped against the wall with his hand rested on the cat. His eyes stare forward into nothing, unfocused.

I go back to him.

"Hey," I say. "Jonah."

He swallows like it takes all the effort in the world.

"It was like in my nightmares, the ones I had after. It was like he picked the scene right out of my head and laid it out in front of me."

"I know."

He doesn't say anything else for a minute, and neither do I.

"You don't have to come tomorrow," I say. "I can go alone. I know what to do now."

Jonah shakes his head. "No way."

"But he—"

"Showed me an accident I've replayed in my head ten million times. In the moment, it felt real. It shocked me. I still can't get the image out of my mind, but I'm not staying here while you go."

I open my mouth.

"Don't argue."

"I could steal your car while you sleep," I say.

"And I know five people off the top of my head who I can call for a ride. We do this together."

Even through the exhaustion in his voice, his demands carry a strength I don't dare contradict. He has as much reason to want to finish this as I do. Maybe more now.

"We got a deal?" he holds a hand out to shake mine.

"I swear to god if you spit in your hand I will vomit in every drawer in this apartment."

I take his hand in mine, squeezing along with him in agreement.

"Now, I'm going to make some emotionally healing macaroni and cheese while you keep researching ..." He glances at the contents of my open backpack. "... whatever it is you've been researching."

"Arson!" I say, faux cheerfully.

CHAPTER

FORTY

The morning greets us with perfect weather for a fire. Cool, dry, and a bit breezy. No rain in sight, despite yesterday's miserable drizzle.

At Roger's house, Jonah stuffs some folded up newspapers into his backpack along with the water and granola bars. I remove a one gallon, red plastic gas can from the back of the Subaru and set it on the lawn. We filled it on the way here.

While Jonah went in the gas station for a handful of the free, local papers, I took his phone and typed a message to the contact labeled Hellie as part of the back up plan I didn't tell him about.

Benjamin will burn today.

Then tomorrow, if I'm lucky, I'll start over for the last time. Third time's the charm, as they say.

We sling the backpacks over our shoulders and I take

up my jug of gasoline. Again, I look away from the barn and ignore the feeling of unease its presence gives off.

"No matter what you see, don't give up the bones," Jonah says. "I won't ask you for them. But Benjamin knows you have them, and he knows what they signify."

"Okay." I find them wrapped in their paper towel in the zippered pocket of my jacket, where I put them.

Neither Jonah nor I speak again as we follow our orange markings through the woods towards Benjamin's altar.

He has to know we're coming by now, and I prepare for whatever he throws at us in an attempt to slow us down.

Jonah and I will be successful. We can do this. I repeat the mantra in my head, leaving no space for the doubt and negativity and fear that dances just barely out of reach.

The forest buzzes around us with electricity, like it knows we've come to remove a cancer from its belly.

I clutch the plastic handle of the gas can tighter and imagine the heat of the blaze we'll create against my cheeks when I watch this nightmare end. It feels wrong to anticipate such violence and destruction. The old me would never have made it to this point, and I don't know what that says about the new me. Killing old ghosts and shit doesn't really fit with what I had in mind a month ago.

The dread comes on gradually, like wading into a lake and feeling the water level rise against your ankles, then your shins and thighs, and then you're fully submerged and clinging to the last breath in your lungs.

Among the sounds of the forest, I hear a familiar sound. A coarse mew with a squeak at the end.

I stop in my tracks and pinch my eyes shut, jam my fingers in my ears even though the weight of the gas can makes it difficult. The sound makes it through, as if it comes from inside my head.

It isn't real. It isn't real. It isn't real.

Another meow, more frantic than the first two.

Beef is not in the woods. Benjamin is responsible for this.

"What is it?" Jonah asks.

"It's nothing."

"I heard a cat."

I shake my head so hard the thoughts might tumble out.

As if on cue, Beef—no, a lookalike—crawls out of a thick tangle of brambles. He has prickly burrs stuck in his gray fur and walks with a limp in one of his back legs.

He calls for me, but I can't go to him. I stand paralyzed in place as he comes towards us, his gait looking mechanical and forced.

It looks so much like him.

But my Beef doesn't move like that. This cat moves towards me like bad CG in a low budget movie. He has a crusty trail of blood smeared from one swollen, half-shut eye to his neck.

"What if I'm wrong?" I whisper. "What if it is Beef and I ignore him thinking it's a trick?"

My voice catches in my throat.

"I can't lose him."

Jonah kneels on the ground and holds a hand out for the cat, but Not-Beef glares at him from a few feet away.

Mentally, I go through my morning. I saw Beef sitting comfortably in the center of Jonah's armchair in his apartment a few miles from here. We shut the door tightly when we left. The windows were locked. Beef couldn't get out unless someone let him out.

"We have to keep walking," I say. "It's not him. It's not my Beef."

If I don't come back, will he understand what happened?

"Ready?" Jonah asks.

I nod.

The cat cries behind us, begging for me to turn and go to him. The sound ricochets in my skull, so clear and familiar.

It takes everything in me to not spin on my heels and rush back.

If Benjamin takes Beef, I won't be able to bounce back. I'll have nothing left. I won't have any reason to keep going.

Tears prick the back of my eyes, and the cold air sends a chill through the dampness collecting in my bottom lids.

Don't think about Beef being gone.

Don't think about it.

A scream builds in my chest, and I clench my fists against the urge to release it.

Don't think about it.

We've only been out here a little over an hour, and Benjamin has already crawled beneath my skin. I have to push him out and take control again.

The cat's desperate pleas fade as we put more distance between us, and I concentrate on breathing. In through the nose, out through the mouth. I ignore the burning in my entire body from the anxiety and exertion.

I shift the gas can from one hand to the other, and shake the stiff bones of the hand that previously white knuckled the handle.

My eyes stay locked on Jonah's back as I put one foot in front of the other until eventually I don't hear the cat anymore. My breathing evens out, and my thoughts stop racing. Only the repeated worry that the animal back there was mine remains, nagging at me like water corroding stone.

When my foot catches a root, I stumble forward and drop the gas can before I can regain my balance. My arms flail in an attempt to recenter myself, but I end up catching myself on the coarse bark of a tree. My hands bleed where the bark tore the skin.

I lean my head against the tree's trunk for a minute, then go retrieve the gas can.

Then I look up to find Jonah ahead of me, but he isn't there anymore.

CHAPTER
FORTY-ONE

"JONAH!" I CALL UNTIL MY THROAT GOES RAW.

He can't have just disappeared like that, but I have no other explanation for how he vanished. Before I fell, we had only a few paces between us. He couldn't have gotten far, but I run for what feels like forever without catching up with him.

The orange paint on the trees tells me the way, and I follow them religiously despite the panic stacking up inside me.

"Jonah." My voice breaks.

How long have I been out here? How close am I to the altar?

Where is Jonah?

I nearly trip again as I rush through the forest in search of him. My legs burn and scream for me to stop. My breath comes in ragged gasps. I can't breathe but I can't stop.

Eventually I lose steam and have to slow down. The

forest seems to thicken around me, but, aside from Jonah being missing, everything feels peaceful and silent. Too peaceful. Too silent.

I cough up phlegm and spit it out on the ground. Breakfast might have been a good idea, but I didn't eat and now my body feels empty, run down. Jonah has all the snacks in his bag, but I have gin. A dry, pitiful laugh escapes me. What fucking good is gin going to do?

My eyes itch, and I rub at them.

After the colorful spots in my vision fade, I catch sight of a figure in the distance. They stand off to the side, off the sad little trail we've made through the wilderness, and I can't see their face. The silhouette of a backpack hung from one shoulder leads me to believe it's Jonah, but I approach slowly.

This could be another trick.

"Marisa, there you are." Jonah's voice is breathy, tired.

I spit out more phlegm, apologizing to him for being disgusting.

"What happened? How'd you get so far ahead?"

He shrugs. "I don't know. I got lost, or you got lost. The path isn't right."

"What? No, it's right. We marked it ourselves."

"No. He made another one to trick us." He points to a tree an arm's length away. "See?"

Around us is a circle of trees marked with orange paint. Each one leads in a different direction.

I rub my eyes again. Is it allergy season already? My nose runs, and my throat feels coated with thick goop. I can't spit enough of it out. It keeps returning, thicker than before.

"I was on the right path. Come with me."

He lets me take his hand and lead him back to the path I'd been following. As much as I want to doubt myself, I don't. This is the right path. Jonah simply got mixed up.

With one hand clutching Jonah's, I lift my hand holding the gas and wipe my nose on my sleeve then rub my eyes with my knuckles.

Something solid comes out, too big to be normal eye crust.

I take my hand back and pick the solid thing off my eye thinking maybe it's a piece of bark or something. Without looking at it, I flick it to the ground.

"What the hell?" Jonah says behind me.

I turn in time to see him rubbing his own eyes. Beneath his hand, I see something long and thin—almost like an eyelash, but wrong.

"What's wrong?" I ask.

He pulls his hand away, and I watch the bottom eyelid of his right eye as something emerges from it. What I thought was an eyelash isn't a part of the human anatomy. The antenna comes out of his eye like it belongs there, followed by the narrow, segmented body and many legs of a house centipede.

I watch in horror as it crawls out of his eye, down his cheek, and falls to his shoulder.

The itch in my nose and my eyes returns, and I feel the solid, segmented bodies emerge from my face as well. First my right eye, then my left nostril, then two crawl out of my mouth. They march down my face and neck with too many feet. In my throat, they choke me so I can't scream.

More come from Jonah too, and he asks me for the gasoline. The look in his eyes, wild and terrified, makes me take a step back as he reaches for the can.

"The centipedes are a nice touch," he says. "I can't tell you've got her all wrong when she's covered in bugs."

I take a step back, stumbling when my heel hits a raised

root. Something—something other than centipedes crawling out of my face—is wrong. Jonah is wrong.

"Give me the gas," he demands. "Or tell me where the real Marisa is."

I can't speak through the bugs crawling in my mouth, so I turn to run.

He lunges at me, and I fall back and drop the gasoline. Only then do I realize he holds the lighter in the hand he hadn't used to rub his face.

I crawl towards the gas can, but a sharp, shooting pain in my tailbone stops me in place.

What do I do?

By the time I regain the ability to breathe, Jonah has the gas can and fiddles with the nozzle.

He looks at me, eyes glinting with disgust and fear, and I know then what I should've known sooner.

This is all a trick.

Benjamin is making me see things. My Jonah is somewhere else, probably seeing visions of his own.

This version means to set me ablaze.

"Where is Marisa?" Not-Jonah demands. "What did you do with her?"

He splashes fuel on the legs of my jeans, then on my coat. It gets in my hair, and the stench of fuel sneaks in my nostrils.

"No!" I beg. "Jonah, it's me. It's really me." I fling another two centipedes off my face, only for them to be replaced with more. They crawl out of my ears, my hair, the collar of my shirt, and their little feet brush my skin like whispered threats. "They're just bugs, Jonah. Please. He's making it seem worse than it is, but it's just bugs."

The lighter doesn't spark a flame, and he grows impatient with it. I take the opportunity to push myself to my feet despite the shock of pain in the lower half of my body. I throw myself at him, hoping to knock the can of gasoline out of his hands and stop him from dousing me any further.

He falls backwards, and the gas can tumbles out of reach. I land on him, struggling to get the lighter away now that the fuel has fallen. He clutches my wrists, trying to throw me off balance so he can overpower me.

This can't be my Jonah.

His eyes contain nothing but rage, as if I'm the thing tormenting him.

"Jonah. No."

He throws me aside with strength I didn't know he had, and I land hard on my back again. He stands, giving me time to rummage through my backpack and dig out the knife, throwing the plastic sheath aside and holding the handle tight in my hand before he comes for me again. His hands reach for my throat, and I close my eyes as the knife plunges beneath his right shoulder when he comes down on me again.

My nose and throat clears like there had never been anything blocking them.

Oh my god.

I stabbed him.

I didn't have a choice.

I stabbed Jonah in the chest.

I roll off him and vomit violently onto the soil, centipedes writhing in the meager contents of my stomach.

FORTY-TWO

A RUSTLING COMES FROM THE BRUSH BEHIND ME AS I stare at Not-Jonah's still breathing body on the ground. His eyes stare up unfocused at the treetops, and his breathing rattles in his chest.

Oh my god.

Panic clutches my entire body at the doubt with in me. It was self defense. This was an illusion. The real Jonah has to be around here somewhere.

I didn't stab my friend. I stabbed someone who looked like him.

Footsteps come closer, and I snatch the lighter from where Jonah dropped it and turn to find the altar behind me. A shadow approaches, shorter and skinnier than Jonah, and my eyes take in a sight so wrong, so unnatural I don't know how to process it.

I press the heels of my hands into my eyes until I see colors, then open them again to find nothing has changed.

A woman, or half of one, stands a few feet away from me in tan pants and a fleece jacket. The clothing is torn and frayed, hanging in ribbons from the remains of her body.

Around me, my vision clears and the illusions disappear. A circle of spruce trees surround me, and the tall stone stands triumphant as always in the center of the blackened clearing.

I have no idea how I got here.

"You're not Benjamin," I say.

The figure reaches for me with a fleshless hand, her skeleton exposed to show what should have been bone but is instead roots. Shreds of muscle hang from the roots, and they tighten as she wiggles her fingers at me—only three and a thumb. Her chest only has half her ribs remaining, while the rest have been replaced with the forest. Thick tendrils of vines weave together to create new bones. Centipedes and spiders and earwigs crawl through the gaps in her skeleton, like they've been working on decomposing her for a long time. In the center of her, a small animal skull sits around a barely beating heart.

"No. I'm not." A gaping opening in her neck reveals the vibration of vocal cords, and they create a voice like a gale.

"You're Evie."

She looks at me, face similar to her chest. Half the skull is gone, showing a brain replaced by an elaborate mush-room cap—red with white spots to indicate poison.

"You came to kill me," she says, examining the stumps on her left hand where the ring finger and pinkie used to be.

I nod.

"I didn't think you would fight back against your friend," she says. "That worries me."

"It wasn't really him. You made him."

Evie laughs, and a spider comes loose from where an ear should be.

"I can't make complete humans. There's too much to a person. Your cat was difficult enough to get right, and I had the walk wrong didn't I?"

"You're lying." She did get Beef's walk wrong.

"You killed your only friend." Evie continues laughing, a madwoman tethered only to her cruelty.

I stand, gasoline in one hand and lighter in the other.

"No." My voice shakes.

Evie goes to Jonah and plucks the knife from his chest. I wince at the spread of blood on his shirt, though I barely got the knife halfway in. His body stiffens against the pain, and he draws in a violent breath.

I can't close my eyes or look away as Evie tosses the knife aside.

We're within the boundary of her prison, blackened grass beneath my boots.

"I can heal his wound," Evie says. "Or you can do what you came here for."

She gestures to the gasoline and lighter in my hand.

"Why are you still here?" I ask. "Where is Benjamin? Who is the other body?"

She grins, a smile made half of teeth and half of the shells of beetles. "Benjamin got to die. And she's ..." Evie waves a hand dismissively at the other corpse. "Betty."

"Benjamin killed her."

"No. They meant to trick me. It was a scheme, because Betty hadn't been content with me. She married him against my wishes, and I objected. She said I was controlling, selfish. A monster. But Benjamin was no better. He had a bad temper and he didn't approve of Betty's and my relationship. He didn't love her half as much as I did, and I knew, the second her car turned up, that he'd killed her. After I took him out here to give him what he deserved, she appeared at my doorstep. Alive.

She demanded to know what I'd done to her husband, and I showed her."

Holy fuck.

"They can be together now, like they wanted. They were weak."

She shows me the scene. Fire rages high off the ground while Betty screams in agony. Benjamin's broken body remains motionless by the stone. Evie stands there in her previous body, hand with the missing fingers wrapped in a bandage.

"You cut off your own fingers. For what?" I grind my teeth against the image she shows me. My head throbs at the effort to dismiss the alternate reality she wants to plunge me into.

"I had to stay and be sure they were gone, like they deserved. Roger was supposed to burn the house down with the last of me, so we'd never be found. He knew I didn't really want him."

"What made you this way?"

"I failed." She shrugs, and a pill bug tumbles from her collarbone. "Betty betrayed me. I gave her everything and she discarded me like garbage. I didn't deserve this. No, I deserved to be happy."

She's too far gone to reason with now. Everything she's done, she believes it was warranted. After all this time, she still thinks she's the hero—or at least a victim—in her story. Benjamin deserved to die because she thought he killed Betty. Betty deserved to die because Evie thought she deserved her love and devotion.

"I don't know what your problem is with me, but I'm not letting you do this to anyone else."

I pat my coat pockets, searching for the lump where I kept the bones. Still there.

"You weren't supposed to be in that house. All I could

feel was your wallowing over a man who didn't even love you in the end. He wasn't even worth the time. Constant misery and anxiety and self pity day in and day out got old fast, especially when you already had someone new willing to die for you. God, it was pathetic. Do you know how sad you have to be to make a ghost depressed?"

Despite the insults, I linger on one part. *You already had someone new willing to die for you.* I glance over to where Not-Jonah had lay, and I hope for a vacant spot to prove it was an illusion.

He remains where I left him, blood spreading over his jacket.

I have to help him. I have to get him out of here.

"Sorry I disturbed your peace and quiet." I spit the words, spiteful and full of hate. This woman can't even accept responsibility for the fact that she's stuck out here, when she should be dead too.

Evie does not seem concerned when I tip the gas can and begin spilling the liquid on the already charred ground. She allows me to walk in a circle, as though she doesn't think I pose a threat. She thinks I won't risk letting Jonah die, assuming the body behind me belongs to the real person. I figure out how to pray just to ask the universe to spare my friend. Please let the man I stabbed be an illusion.

But even if he really lies bleeding behind me, I know he'd want me to finish this. If it's really Jonah that I stabbed, I have to end this for him.

So I let her think I'm bluffing.

If only a seed of doubt weren't growing within me. She knows what I know. She knows I have the bones and the gasoline.

Why isn't she worried?

I walk toward the altar and spill gasoline in a ring

around it, focusing extra on the pile of bones at the foot of the stone.

"If I die, he dies," Evie says. "You can't have both of the things you want. You're too weak to carry him all the way back without the fire taking you both, especially with all that fuel on your clothes. Will you really let him die? Would you really risk leaving your cat an orphan?"

My heart breaks in half as I think of the text I sent Hellie from Jonah's phone.

> **Jonah:**
> Marisa and I are dealing with something urgent. If you don't hear from me by tonight, can you take her cat for a couple days? His name is Beef. He's at my apartment.

She read it within a minute. Accepted the responsibility shortly after.

She and Jack will take good care of him.

"No. I wouldn't leave him, and I won't leave Jonah."

I flick the lighter three times before it produces a flame. What remains of Evie's expression changes to fear as I touch the fire to the gasoline soaked heap of bones and it goes up in flames with a whoosh. Branches and tree bark fallen from nearby trees make perfect kindling, and the fire rises rapidly.

Evie's form flickers as she screams in agony. I drag Jonah out of immediate danger, then watch as Evie's body —if it can even be called that—is unmade like it should have been decades ago.

Pieces of nature fall away from her. Insects fly off her like sparks, and the wood within her skeleton twists and pops from the heat. She screams. Then she goes silent and kneels in the center of the inferno I've created in only a matter of minutes.

Next, I pull the gin out of my bag and throw it into the center of the blaze. The bottle smashes in a ball of fire. Then comes the plastic bottle of lighter fluid.

Illusions flicker around me as Evie tries fighting. A poorly rendered Beef appears in a corner, then wavers and pops up somewhere else. The mangled snowmobile flashes before me. A body. Voices float around my head—Brent's and Jonah's and Elise's, all begging me to save them. Taunting me.

I place the finger bones on the ground at the edge of the circle just as the fire catches the ends of the branches of the spruce trees. The boundary doesn't stop the flames from spreading, and it rushes outwards.

FORTY-THREE

"MARISA?" A WEAK VOICE CREAKS OVER THE SOUND OF crackling flames.

I turn to Jonah's body and he's propped himself up against a rock. His right arm hangs limp at his side. Unlike the other illusions Evie tries to sustain as she dies, the image of Jonah remains solid.

"Jonah. Are you you?"

He tries to nod.

Evie wasn't lying.

Oh my god.

My hands quake, and I notice the smear of blood on the hand that held the knife. I did this. I stabbed Jonah.

"No. No, no, no."

Panicked, I rush to his side and try to stop the bleeding.

"I'm so sorry, Jonah. I thought ..." I can't explain myself.

His eyelids flutter.

"Can you … can you walk?" I ask. I can't believe I have the audacity to ask the man I stabbed if he can walk.

He pushes himself up more with his left arm, and together we manage to get him upright. Behind me, the flames catch a dead tree outside the now-charred circle of spruces and the fire rips through a pile of yellowed pine needles. The gasoline on my clothes stings my nose, reminding me it's there.

"I'll get you out of this," I say as I guide him forward.

It might be a lie.

We stumble through the forest, my legs weak from the extra weight of Jonah's injured body. The whole forest reeks of smoke, and my lungs fill with it until I can't breathe anymore. My head swims from lack of oxygen, and I cough so hard my ribs scream.

My eyes sting and I can barely make out the orange blazes we left on the trees. I could be going the wrong way, deeper into the forest and farther from home.

How much time has passed? Has Hellie gone to retrieve Beef yet? I can hardly think, let alone process the numbers on the screen of the phone I pulled from the front of Jonah's backpack, which I left behind. I stare at the phone, letting Jonah rest against a tree for a minute.

A text from Hellie waits on the screen.

Hellie:

Where are you?

Jonah you need to text me.

She's already there. My eyes fill with tears of relief. Beef will be okay. At least I didn't fail him too.

The phone starts to ring but I can't answer it because I don't think I can speak. My throat feels so raw.

I open the text thread with Hellie and send our location.

Jonah:
SOS

With the message sent and delivered, my body turns to lead. I fall to my knees, then to the ground.

Beside me, I hear a thud as Jonah collapses beside me.

The touch of his fingers on mine is the last thing I feel before I let go.

CHAPTER

FORTY-FOUR

THE WORLD AROUND ME IS HAZY, SMOKY AS I MOVE TOO fast through the forest. The humming of an engine grates against my brain like a hammer and chisel, and if I could talk I'd tell the person responsible for the noise to stop and let me die in peace.

I see trees.

Darkness.

Smoke.

Darkness.

More trees.

My head lolls back and forth with the motion of the machine carrying me through the forest. A motorcycle? I don't know.

The heat from the fire licks my skin. The smoke stings my eyes.

Every inch of me is filthy, covered in ash and smoke. In gasoline and someone else's blood.

More darkness fills my vision. A voice comes from somewhere near me, but I don't comprehend the language.

An image of Beef pops into my head.

Then of Jonah with a pink kitchen knife sticking out of his chest.

Evie.

Fire.

So much fire.

The screen of the phone with text dripping like watercolor as I messaged Hellie.

I killed Jonah.

I'm not dead.

I think I want to be.

But I'm not dead.

FORTY-FIVE

I wake up in my bed in Wisconsin with Beef curled behind the bend in my knees. It smells like something burning, and I rise to investigate.

Beyond the bedroom, I step into Roger's living room. Beef sits on the couch.

I blink, and the room goes sideways. I grip the floor as it rotates upright, and I slide until the soles of my boots make contact with the wall beneath.

The setting changes. Wisconsin. Roger's house. Jonah's apartment.

The hospital dad died in.

This isn't real.

Jonah enters through the solid floor. He wears his work vest and holds two bottles of lighter fluid in one hand. His eye sockets are dark pits filled with writhing centipedes.

Blood drips from an injury on his right shoulder,

creating a path of damp red from underneath his vest to the thighs of his jeans.

Another change in the scene and the two of us are back in the woods, Jonah with a knife in his chest and me with my fist tight around the handle.

I push it in deeper.

Warm liquid bubbles up on the heel of my hand.

Evie killed Benjamin, then she killed Betty.

I killed Jonah.

Evie laughs somewhere in the distance, then it turns into a scream.

This isn't real.

I know it isn't, because reality doesn't work like this. The edges of Evie's illusion flicker and break. She doesn't have the strength she once did. The heat of the flames must be incinerating her.

I killed Jonah.

My head aches from smoke inhalation. My lungs are filled with dirty clouds.

I envision the tiny scavengers that crawled inside her body fleeing, desperately trying to escape the flames as the nature within her caught fire.

Voices swirl around me.

Beef meows.

The imagined sensation of the cat's soft fur on my hand brings me a second of comfort, even if it's fake. I don't care.

The frantic beeping of machinery scares the cat away. It drives a blade straight through the center of my skull, cleaving my brain in two.

"Are they going to be okay?" a voice asks from a mile away.

My eyelids grow heavy and fall closed, leaving me to fade into the dark while the beeping machines scream me a lullaby.

FORTY-SIX

In the hospital, I ask about Beef. I ask about Jonah. I ask about what happened.

In that order.

"Your cat is okay. Hellie and Jack Holland informed us they've taken him in while you're here."

I cry with momentary relief, but the tears make my eyes burn.

"As for you, you've got burns on your legs and hands, and you inhaled a lot of smoke. You'll be okay, though. You're very lucky to have gotten out of there." The voice that responds belongs to someone I don't know. "It was a bad fire."

"What about Jonah?"

My eyes focus on a young, Black nurse in sunshine yellow scrubs and her hair tucked away in a matching wrap. Her badge reads 'Courtney' in letters that appear to drip down the white plastic.

She looks at me with a gentle expression.

"I don't know."

Beeping comes from all around me. I swear my ears are bleeding from all the noise.

I bark a gritty cough. The substance in my throat reminds me of the mud Benjamin—no, Evie—made me feel in my throat. When I cover my mouth with a hand, I half expect to find a centipede. Instead, only ash and dirt soiled saliva.

"How did we get here?"

A lightness fills my head and makes the room spin when I try sitting up, and the nurse tells me to take it easy. I can't.

"Hellie called emergency services after she got a text from Jonah. Volunteer firefighters got out there on ATVs and pulled you both out."

The memory of sending the text to Hellie with our location is muted and soft at the edges. It hangs back in my mind like a scene from something I'd seen, and not like something I'd done myself. It doesn't fit with the other things in my head.

Evie made me see so much, every time I think about the events in the woods, it goes as well as trying to make a picture from pieces of two different puzzles. None of it matches up. The lines are all jagged. The colors are all wrong.

"Did they find anything in the barn?" I ask, knowing they didn't. There was no horse, but I ache for confirmation.

"What barn?" the nurse asks.

"The one on Roger's property. By the house where I was living."

The nurse screws up her face. "Marisa, honey. You need to rest now," the nurse says, avoiding my question. "I will check on you later, and I will have an update about your friend."

"No. Wait. Please tell me about the barn," I demand. "What did they find?"

The nurse sighs, but gives in. "That barn burned down eight years ago and was not rebuilt."

The words hit me like a punch in the stomach. At some point, these things should stop shocking me, but I guess I haven't gotten there yet. It would be in my best interest to assume nothing from the last two weeks was real. That everything was an elaborate hallucination.

"Please rest. You need it."

I do as she says, if only because sleep will pass the time before I learn the extent of what I've done.

FORTY-SEVEN

The police should question me.

After all, I did stab someone in the process of being present for a wildfire that tore through the forest behind the house I lived in. A house that also burned down.

I prepare my story for them, knowing they won't believe me. They'll think I've made everything up, and they'll send me for a psychological evaluation. I know they'll send me to prison. If Jonah's dead—and maybe even if he's still alive— there won't be anyone to be disappointed or miss me while I spend the rest of my life behind bars.

But the cops don't arrive and immediately read me my rights. They don't arrive at all.

Hellie and Jack visit some time after the nurse informs me that Jonah will survive.

They look at me with sympathy I don't deserve.

"We know what the two of you were doing out there," Jack says.

It doesn't come out like a reprimand, only a fact. He knows.

"Jonah is exceptionally bad at a few things," Jack continues. "One is carrying things appropriately. Another is keeping secrets."

Hellie looks exhausted, with dark circles under her eyes. I notice an angry red scratch across one of her hands when she reaches to rub her eyes. God damnit, Beef. I owe these people so much.

"We knew you two decided to explore the local legend about Eveline Ouellette. Hellie asked him how he felt about spending time in that house, and you should have seen him sweat. The boy has no pokerface. No ability to lie. None of that."

"Why are you telling me this?" I ask, unable to follow the conversation.

"The fire was investigated, and the authorities decided the cause was Eveline Ouellette trying to dispose of the bodies of two people she killed two decades ago."

Jack leans forward in the uncomfortable looking hospital chair.

"Jonah said he doesn't remember how he got the stab wound."

I nod. Shocked.

"All of this works out to be a big, freak accident in which the two of you are doing god knows what in the woods and somehow in the process you find the remains of the most infamous people in Bowen's Leg history."

How is this happening?

"Did they identify the remains?" I ask. "And how they died?"

Hellie nods. "Eveline died in the fire. The other two are still being investigated."

The back of my head sinks deeper into the pillow

beneath me. Evie hadn't been dead when I saw her, but she certainly hadn't been alive either. Could she have been hiding her real appearance from me?

I don't ask the question out loud.

Hellie and Jack don't need to know what she looked like to me.

It's better, maybe, that everyone rules curses and magic out. The truth is too far out there. People don't need to know what really happened here, because people are prone to bad ideas.

"So that's it, then?" I ask. "The case is closed."

"That's it."

"Thank you," I say. "Is Beef doing okay?"

We drop the subject of local legends and Hellie tells me everything Beef has done in the few hours since she retrieved him from Jonah's apartment. Despite the scratches on her hand, she seems enamored by him.

Knowing he's okay and that Jonah will live allows me to finally really rest. Hellie and Jack leave me to go back to sleep, and, despite everything, I slip into the type of sleep that comes only with peace.

FORTY-EIGHT

I GET SICK OF TELLING THE "OFFICIAL" STORY ABOUT finding Evie after the first half dozen interviews. Jonah doesn't show up to any of them, so I sit alone and face the reporters, the bloggers, the people from podcasts and true crime YouTube series. When people ask about him, I can't comment beyond my script. No one asked me not to, but given the fact that I haven't heard from him since we left the hospital, I get the sense he doesn't want to be a part of this.

The least I can do is entertain all the people with questions until they lose interest, and spare him the unwanted attention.

Of all the lies I say into cell phone microphones, the one about how Jonah got stabbed is the hardest.

Officially, Evie stabbed him, because, officially, we stumbled upon her in the act of moving the bodies from a decades old crime. She tried to get away. Jonah tried to stop her. He got stabbed. She fell and hit her head, which is what led to her being killed in the fire.

Without Jonah, I don't have anyone to talk to about what really happened, and it eats at me like the things I saw crawling through what remained of Evie's body.

Hellie and Jack set me up in their guest room, since Roger's house burned with several miles of forest. Technically, the guest room had been the dogs' room, and Peony and Lilac are less than impressed by the fact that I've taken their bed. In protest, the two of them team up with Beef to take up half the queen sized bed each night.

I remember so much.

I wish I could forget all of it.

On the nights when I do sleep, I wake to the feeling of insects in my eyes and throat, or of plunging a knife into my friend. I didn't even get a chance to apologize. No, I didn't take the chances I got. I live with Hellie and Jack, but don't venture out of my room when he comes to see them. He doesn't come upstairs, though I've heard him talking to Beef from the floor below. I've felt his presence within mere feet of me, and I haven't been brave enough to face him.

TWO MONTHS PASS BEFORE WE TALK AGAIN.

I drink coffee at the kitchen island while Jack makes a "Sunday Scramble" for the dogs and cat, which is just scrambled eggs from their chickens. Jonah wanders in as I watch Beef devour his breakfast, then attempt to stealthily move over and stick his head in Peony's bowl.

"Oh. Hi," he says. "I thought you'd be upstairs."

I shake my head. "Nope." Before, I'd tell him about the job interview I have scheduled in two hours. He'd tell me about something equally riveting. We'd make jokes at one another's expense.

He shrugs. Jack pours him a cup of coffee, then goes outside to leave us alone.

"How are things?" he shifts his weight from one foot to the other, then back again.

"They're okay. You?"

Awkward. So awkward. How is this the same guy I knew before?

"I've been kind of a jerk," he says.

I meet his eyes and take on the weight of the pain he carries in them. His hair has grown longer, and the stubble on his chin has grown into a neat beard. For the first time since I met him, he isn't wearing flannel or his work vest. He wears a charcoal colored button down with jeans that look new and a pair of clean boots, an ensemble that gives off job interview vibes.

"I shouldn't have avoided you after the hospital," he continues. "I wasn't sure what to say, and then I stopped trying to figure it out."

"I'm sorry I stabbed you," I blurt.

He absently touches the place I imagine the scar to be. "I'm sorry you needed to."

"I should have tried harder to get away or fight you off without resorting to that."

"You had no choice!"

I shake my head. "I did…"

"I tried to kill you." His voice is no more than a whisper, like it's the first time he's acknowledged what happened in those woods aloud.

"I remember the knife going in. I see it every time I close my eyes."

"Let yourself forget."

We drink our coffee in silence for a few minutes while we figure out what to say next.

"Can we start over?" he asks.

I shake my head, and Jonah's face falls.

"That's not how things work in real life," I say.

When I came here, I lied to myself and said it would be a fresh start. I told myself I could redefine myself despite everything I experienced beforehand. New beginnings don't exist. We have to pick up where we left off and build something from the wreckage.

"We're stuck with the memory of what happened, all of it. That doesn't mean we can't keep being friends—I want to be friends, or whatever—it just means we have to acknowledge all the ways we fucked up before we keep going. The stabbing. Whatever Evie made you see when you poured gasoline on me. We have to talk about that if we want to stay in one another's lives." I leave the final choice up to him, because I can't bring myself to be vulnerable right now. I can't bear to be denied.

ANOTHER MONTH PASSES, AND JONAH AND I SIT opposite one another at a high-top at the Wobbly Leg. We eat godawful bar food and chase it with decent beer. We make wildly inappropriate jokes about stab wounds, as if he hadn't actually experienced one at my hand. It feels almost normal to be together like this again, talking about my eight million job interviews, and his meetings with a town council that barely functioned prior to all this.

It feels like maybe we could be okay.

CHAPTER

FORTY-NINE

PEOPLE LEAVE US ALONE. THE CASE FADES OUT OF FOCUS now that everyone has told their version of the story.

Nobody cares about the two people in the small, barely on the map town in Maine who apparently solved a decades old mystery. We sink into a relationship unburdened by the weight of a curse. A relationship I might've seen coming if we hadn't been so distracted before.

Jonah stands in the doorway of my room at Hellie and Jack's with a stupid grin on his face. He holds a giant iced coffee, a whoopie pie, and a giant, sparkly balloon that reads Happy First Birthday with the word 'Birth' poorly crossed out with what appears to be permanent marker.

"I don't love that I can't show up at your workplace and embarrass you on your first day, so I had to settle."

I sit at a desk facing a company issued laptop from a tech company that designs dating apps. Of all people, they hired *me* as a project manager, and my first assignment is

268

working on a special app to help divorcees get back on their feet in a new world of dating. Objectively hilarious, considering I skipped over the Dating-As-A-Divorced-Adult phase and moved straight into a slow burn relationship with the first person whose butt I ogled as a single woman.

It was probably inevitable I'd end up with Jonah, though we both had to work out the whole stabbing thing with our respective therapists.

"Happy first … birthday?" I quirk an eyebrow.

"It's Bowen's Leg. Pickings were slim."

The balloon fits how I feel, though I hit my 27th birthday two weeks ago. This is what I wanted. A surprisingly decent job, weekly therapy, a shiny, zippy little Hyundai no one owned before me, and a place to live that feels closer to home than any place I've been in a while. Though, I won't live in Hellie and Jack's guest room forever.

"You're a dork," I say as the laptop pings with a calendar reminder for a meeting that starts in fifteen minutes. "Okay, I have to do this shit."

He brings the coffee and whoopie pie to me, then ties the balloon to the back of my chair. I pull up the invite to the virtual orientation that starts in five minutes. He plants a kiss on my cheek, then closes the door quietly behind him as he leaves.

I suck in a breath, then close my eyes as it leaves my lungs.

I've broken curses. I've overcome nightmares. I've rebuilt my life.

A job at a dating app company will be a piece of cake.